Tanya drew a blue line of sky at the top of the
page, and then right above my head she did a big
yellow sun with rays all around it. Then she
wrote a title at the top. Her writing was rather
wobbly and I knew she'd spelled a word wrong
but it didn't matter a bit.

MY FREND MANDY

That's what she wrote. And I felt so happy I felt
as if there was a real sun above my head and I
was dancing in its warm yellow rays . . .

Bad Girls is Jacqueline Wilson's eighth title to
be published by Corgi Yearling Books. Her
previous books include *The Suitcase Kid*, which
won the 1993 Children's Book Award, and
Double Act, which won both the Smarties Prize
and the Children's Book Award in 1995.

www.kidsatrandomhouse.co.uk

BAD GIRLS

Jacqueline Wilson

ILLUSTRATED BY NICK SHARRATT

CORGI YEARLING BOOKS

BAD GIRLS

A CORGI YEARLING BOOK : 0 440 86777 0

First published in Great Britain by Doubleday,

PRINTING HISTORY
Doubleday edition published 1996
Corgi Yearling edition published 1997

29 30

Corgi Books are published by Random House Children's Books,
61–63 Uxbridge Road, Ealing, London W5 5SA,
a division of The Random House Group Ltd,
in Australia by Random House Australia (Pty) Ltd,
20 Alfred Street, Milsons Point, Sydney, NSW 2061, Australia,
in New Zealand by Random House New Zealand Ltd,
18 Poland Road, Glenfield, Auckland 10, New Zealand
and in South Africa by Random House (Pty) Ltd,
Isle of Houghton, Corner of Boundary Road & Carse O'Gowrie,
Houghton 2198, South Africa

Printed and bound in Great Britain by
Cox & Wyman Ltd, Reading, Berkshire.

For Rebecca Hillman,
special friend
and fellow writer

RED

Red

They were going to get me.

I saw them the moment I turned the corner. They were halfway down, waiting near the bus stop. Melanie, Sarah and Kim. Kim, the worst one of all.

I didn't know what to do. I took a step forward, my sandal sticking to the pavement.

They were nudging each other. They'd spotted me.

I couldn't see that far, even with my glasses, but I knew Kim would have that great big smile on her face.

I stood still. I looked over my shoulder. Perhaps I could run back to school? I'd hung around for ages already. Maybe they'd locked the playground gates? But perhaps one of the teachers would still be there? I could pretend I had a stomachache or something and then maybe I'd get a lift in their car?

'Look at Mandy! She's going to go rushing back to school. *Baby!*' Kim yelled.

She seemed to have her own magic glasses that let her see right inside my head. She didn't wear ordinary glasses, of course. Girls like Kim never wear glasses or braces on their teeth. They never get fat. They never have a silly haircut. They never wear stupid baby clothes.

If I ran back they'd only run after me. So I went on walking, even though my legs were wobbly. I was getting near enough to see them properly. Kim was smiling all right. They all were.

I tried to think what to do.

Daddy told me to try teasing her back. But you can't tease girls like Kim. There's nothing to tease her about.

Mum said just ignore them and then they'll get tired of teasing.

They hadn't got tired yet.

I was getting nearer and nearer. My sandals were still sticking. I was sticking, too. My dress stuck to my back. My forehead was wet under my fringe.

But I tried very hard to look cool. I tried to stare straight past them. Arthur King was waiting at the bus stop. I stared at him instead. He was reading a book. He was always reading books.

I like reading too. It was a shame Arthur King was a boy. And a bit weird. Otherwise we might have been friends.

I didn't have any proper friends now. I used to have Melanie, but then she got friendly with Sarah. Then Kim decided she'd have them in her gang.

Melanie always said she hated Kim. But now she was her best friend. If Kim wants you as a friend then that's it. You don't argue with her. She can be so scary.

She was right in front of me now. I couldn't stare past her any more. I had to look at her. Her bright black eyes and her glossy hair and her big mouth smiling, showing all her white teeth.

I could even see her when I shut my eyes. It was as if she'd stepped through my glasses, straight into my head. Smiling and smiling.

'She's got her eyes shut. Hey, let's bump into her,' said Kim.

I opened my eyes up quick.

'She's mad,' said Sarah.

'She's playing one of her pretend games,' said Melanie.

They all cracked up laughing.

I couldn't stand it that Melanie had told them all our private games. My eyes started

4

stinging. I blinked hard. I knew I mustn't cry no matter what.

Ignore them, ignore them, ignore them . . .

'She's trying to ignore us!' said Kim triumphantly. 'Did Mumsie-Wumsie tell you to ignore us rude nasty girlies, then?'

There was no point trying to ignore her any more. I couldn't, anyway. She'd stepped straight in front of me. She had Melanie on one side, Sarah on the other. I was surrounded.

I swallowed. Kim went on smiling.

'Where *is* Mumsie, anyway?' she said. 'Not like Mumsie to let little Mandy mince home all by herself. We were looking out for her, weren't we, Mel, weren't we, Sarah?'

They always nudged each other and whispered and giggled when my mum went past. They nudged and whispered and giggled even more when Mum and I were together. One terrible time Mum took hold of my hand and they all saw before I could snatch it away. They went on about it for weeks. Kim made up tales of toddler reins and pushchairs and baby bottles. And a dummy for the dummy.

They were nudging and whispering and giggling now. I didn't answer Kim. I tried to dodge round her but she dodged too, so she was standing in front of me. Right up close. Bigger than me.

'Hey, I'm talking to you! You deaf or something? Had I better shout?' said Kim. She bent so close her silky black hair brushed my cheek. 'WHERE'S MUMSIE?' she bellowed into my ear.

I could feel her voice roaring right through my head, whirling up and down every little squiggle of my brain. I peered round desperately. Arthur King was looking up from his book, staring.

I couldn't stand him seeing. I tried hard to pretend that everything was completely normal.

'My mum's at the dentist's,' I said, acting as if Kim and I were having a completely ordinary conversation.

Melanie and Sarah started sniggering. Kim smiled on steadily.

'Oooh, at the *dentist's*,' she said. She sounded as if she was chatting, too. 'Mmm, yes, well, your mum would have to go to the dentist's, wouldn't she, Mandy?' She waited.

I didn't know whether to say anything or not. I waited, too.

'Your mum jolly well needs to go to the

dentist's,' said Kim. 'She's so wrinkly and grey and ancient I expect all her own teeth are crumbling right away. Gone for a full set of false choppers, has she, Mandy?'

 She smiled sweetly as she said it, baring her own perfect teeth. It felt as if she were biting me with them. Cruel little nips, again and again.

'You shut up about my mum,' I said. I meant it to sound threatening but it came out like I was pleading. Either way it wouldn't make any difference. No-one could ever shut Kim up when she got started. Especially not me.

'Your mum looks older than my grandma,' said Kim. 'No, she looks older than my great-grandma. How old was she when she had you, Mandy? Sixty? Seventy? A hundred?'

'You're just being stupid,' I said. 'My mum's not that old.'

'So how old is she, then?'

'It's none of your business,' I said.

'She's fifty-five,' said Melanie. 'And her dad's even older, he's sixty-two.'

I felt my face flushing deep red. I'd told her when we were best friends and she had sworn she'd never ever tell.

'That's *ancient*!' said Sarah. '*My* mum's only thirty-one.'

They all started miming aged old ladies, smacking their lips together and hobbling wide-legged.

'Stop it!' I said, and my glasses started to go smeary. I could still see Arthur King through them. He'd gone back to his book, but his face was red, too.

'Oooh, Mumsie's little pet sugar lump is throwing a wobbly,' said Kim. She stopped clowning and put her arm round Melanie. 'So what's Daddy like then? Is he all googly-eyed and ga-ga?'

'He's got this silly beard and he wears a smock,' said Melanie, and she looked thrilled when Kim hugged her gleefully.

'A *smock*! Like a frock? Mandy's dad wears a *frock*!' Kim yelled, and they all doubled up laughing.

'A smock *isn't* a frock,' I gabbled desperately. 'And it's a man's smock, a fisherman's smock; Daddy just wears it when he's painting.'

'*Daddy!*' They all shrieked again.

My face felt as if it were on fire. I didn't know how the Daddy had slipped out. I tried so hard to say Mum and Dad like all the others. I thought Daddy's smock looked a bit silly too. And I wished my mum didn't have grey hair and a big bulky body that strained tight against her cotton frocks and puffy feet strapped into sandals. I wished my mum was young and cool and pretty like all the other mums. I wished my dad was young and strong and swung me around in the air like the other dads.

I wished it so badly that sometimes at night in bed I pretended I was adopted and that one day my real mum and dad would come and take me away. They'd be ever so young and hip and stylish and they'd let me wear all the latest fashions and play music really loud and eat at McDonald's and they'd let me go round by myself and stay out ever so late and never ever get cross. I'd fall asleep making up all these things about this real mum and dad – I called them by their first names, Kate and Nick, neat, *now* names – and I'd dream about them too, but nearly always, halfway through a dream, when I'd got to the very best bit and Kate and Nick and I were dashing off to Disneyland or checking out the Hard Rock Café, my own mum and dad would suddenly bob up out of nowhere.

They'd generally look even older and more anxious, and they'd be calling for me frantically. I'd pretend not to hear and run off with Kate and Nick, but I'd look back and see them crumpling, starting to cry.

I'd wake up in the morning feeling so guilty that I'd jump straight up when the alarm went and go downstairs to make them a cup of tea, and while they sipped sleepily I'd slide into bed

with them and they'd call me their good little girl. Even though I'm getting big now. And I'm not good, not always. I can be really bad.

'Yes, well, all right, I have to call them Daddy and Mummy because they make me. But they're not my real mum and dad,' someone blurted out. It seemed to be my mouth saying it before I could stop it. It startled me and it startled them too, even Kim.

They stared at me. Arthur King behind them at the bus stop was staring too.

'What are you on about?' said Kim, putting her hands on her hips. Her T-shirt was pulled

tight against her flat stomach.
She was the skinniest girl in
the class, and one of the tallest
too. She said she was going
to be a fashion model when
she was sixteen. Melanie and
Sarah said they were too, but they weren't even
pretty.

I didn't know what I wanted to be when I
grew up. I just wanted to stop being me. I
wanted to grow up a whole new person, not
Mandy White.

'They're not my mum and dad, and my real
name's not Mandy White,' I said. 'It's meant to
be a secret. I was adopted when I was a baby.
I've met my real mum, and she's amazing: she's
a fashion model, she's got this fantastic figure,
she's been in a lot of the papers actually, you'd
know her if I said her name but I'm not allowed,
anyway, she had me very young and it was
going to interfere with her career, so she had
me adopted but she's always regretted it so she
keeps in touch. It upsets my adopted mum and
dad but they can't stop her and she keeps
sending me wonderful presents, all sorts of
clothes and fashionable shoes and stuff, but my
adopted mum doesn't approve and locks them
away in trunks and makes me wear all this
baby stuff . . .' It was getting easier and easier,
the story spinning out of my mouth like silk

thread, and I was embroidering as I went, making it as detailed as possible. They were all listening, all believing me. Sarah's mouth was hanging open and even Kim looked impressed.

I'd forgotten Melanie.

Her head suddenly jerked.

'You liar!' she said. 'That's not true, none of it's true. I've been round to your house, I know your mum and dad, and they're your *real* mum and dad, and there aren't any trunks, and—'

'The trunks are kept up in the loft, see. It *is* true, I swear it is,' I insisted.

'Um, you shouldn't swear on it,' said Melanie. 'Because I *know* it's all a lie. When your mum came round to collect you when you were at my house, she had a cup of coffee with my mum and she went on and on about you, and how she'd had all this yucky fertility treatment for ages and they'd given up all hope of ever having a baby and she said they'd tried to adopt but they were too old but then your mum suddenly started you. "Our little miracle baby."

That's what she said. My mum told me. So you're a *liar*!'

'Liar!' said Kim, but for some strange reason she still looked impressed. Her eyes flickered and I almost dared hope that she'd stop now, that she'd let me go.

I don't know whether I moved or not, edging one half-step sideways. But it was half a step too much.

'Oh, no, you're not going just yet, Mandy Miracle-Babe Loony-Liar,' said Kim.

'Liar,' said Melanie, her head nodding.

'Liar, liar, pants-on-fire,' said Sarah.

They all giggled at the word pants.

'Yeah, what colour pants have you got on today, Mandy?' said Kim, suddenly tugging at my skirt, whipping it up.

'Stop it, stop it,' I said, frantic, clutching it.

But Kim still saw.

'Oh how *sweet*,' she said 'White with little weeny rabbits on! To match the itsy-bitsy bunnies Mumsie knitted on your cardi.' She flicked the rabbits with her long hard fingers.

'Poor Mumsie, knitting and knitting for naughty Miracle-Mandy – when she goes round telling everyone she's adopted! Mumsie's going to be soooooooo upset when she finds out.'

I felt as if she'd flicked a hole right through my stomach.

'How will she find out?' I said hoarsely.

'Well, we'll try asking her. Tomorrow, when she comes to collect you. "How old was Mandy when you adopted her, Mrs White?" I'll say, and she'll say, "Oh, Mandy's my own little girl, dear" and I'll say, "That's not what Mandy says, *she* swears she's adopted",' said Kim, her eyes gleaming.

Melanie and Sarah giggled uncertainly, not sure whether Kim was joking.

I was sure she was deadly serious. I could see her saying it. I could see Mummy's face. I couldn't stand it.

'You're wicked, wicked, wicked!' I shouted and I slapped Kim's face hard.

She was a lot taller than me but my arm reached up of its own accord and my palm caught her cheek. It went bright red, though her other cheek was white. Her eyes went even darker.

'Right,' she said, and she stepped forward.

I knew I was for it now. I shoved Sarah out the way, I dived past Melanie, I dashed out into

the road to get away from Kim because I knew
she was going to kill me.

There was a big blur of red and a shriek of
brakes. I saw the bus. I screamed. And then I
fell.

ORANGE

Orange

'Mandy! Oh my goodness! She's dead!'

I opened my eyes.

'No, I'm not,' I said shakily.

Arthur King was bending over me, his glasses lopsided, his mouth lopsided too, gaping open in shock. More people gathered in a ring around me. One woman knelt down beside me. They were all in a fog. I blinked, but everything stayed blurred.

I struggled to sit up.

'No, dear, you must lie still until the ambulance gets here,' said the kneeling woman. 'The bus driver's phoning for one now.'

An ambulance! Was I badly hurt? I twitched my arms and legs. They seemed to move about normally enough. I felt my head to see if there were any bumps. My hand hurt as I lifted it, pain tweaking up to my elbow.

'Just take it easy, dear. Now then, tell me your name and address so we can let your mother know,' said the woman.

'She's Mandy White. She's in my class at school,' said Arthur King.

'Were you one of those wicked children chasing her?' said the woman indignantly. 'I saw! I was right at the front of the bus and I saw them chase her into the road. She could have been killed.'

'I thought she *was* killed,' said Arthur, shivering. 'I should have stopped them.'

'It wasn't you,' I said. I looked up at the woman. 'It wasn't him.'

'It wasn't the boy, it was those girls,' said someone else.

Everyone turned round. But Kim and Melanie and Sarah had gone.

'Tormenting her. And she's only a little kid too! How old are you dearie, eight?'

'I'm ten,' I said. 'Eleven next month, actually.'

'Where do you live, Mandy?' asked the woman.

'Fifty-six Woodside Road. But please, I'm

OK, you don't need to tell my mum. She'd get ever so worried. And she's not at home anyway, she's at the dentist,' I said, trying to sit up again.

I still couldn't see properly. Then I suddenly realized why.

'My glasses!'

'I've got them here, Mandy. But they've snapped in two,' said Arthur. 'Shall I put them in your pocket?'

'How's the little girl?' said the bus driver, steering Arthur King to one side and bending down beside me.

'I'm all right,' I said shakily, worrying about my broken glasses.

'The ambulance should be here any minute. You look OK to me, but you need to get checked over. They'll take you to the hospital and someone will let your mum know.'

'I'll do that,' said the woman, nodding.

'*No*,' I said, and I burst into tears.

'There, now. It's the shock.'

'I feel like I'm in shock too,' said the bus driver. 'They all suddenly charged into the road, this little one, and then them others, and there was nothing I could do. Lucky job I'd slowed right down because I was nearly at the bus stop. I just bumped her, though. I think she fainted, I don't think she was knocked out.'

'I thought she'd died. She just dropped and

she didn't move,' said Arthur, and his bony fingers felt their way past the kneeling woman and the bus driver and found my hand. 'Don't cry, Mandy. You are really going to be all right, aren't you?' he said.

I couldn't stop crying to say anything and my hand was starting to hurt so much I couldn't even squeeze his fingers. They elbowed him right out of the way when the ambulance came and then I was carried away, even though all I wanted to do was to run home. I tried to stop acting like a big baby, crying like that. I didn't have a hankie and my nose was running horribly right down to my lip, but the kind ambulance woman gave me a tissue and she put her arm round me and told me to cheer up, chicken. She even made clucky hen noises to make me laugh.

Then we got to the hospital and I got scared again because I'd never been in hospital before, and when you see it on television there are always people shouting and covered in blood, and tables where they open you up and there are all your insides glistening in jelly.

Only it wasn't like that a bit. There was just a waiting-room and a lot of people sitting on chairs. I was put

20

in a little cubicle and a nurse came to talk to me because I was on my own. Then a doctor came and prodded me and shone a light in my eyes, and then I was taken to be X-rayed and that didn't hurt a bit though I had to keep still. The radiographer told me how the X-ray machine worked and I asked some more questions and she said I was a clever girl. I was almost starting to enjoy myself. Then I went back to the cubicle to wait for the X-rays to be developed and suddenly I heard Mum calling. Then she came rushing into the cubicle, her face grey, her cheek all puffy from the dentist's injections.

'Oh, Mandy!' she said, and she scooped me into her arms.

It was stupid, but I started crying all over again, and she rocked me as if I was a real baby.

'There, now. It's OK. Mummy's here.'

I burrowed against her soft front and smelt her warm toast-and-talcum smell. I felt so bad about telling Kim and the others that she wasn't my real mum that I cried harder.

'Hang on, poppet. I'm going to get a nurse.

They must give you something to stop the pain. You never make a fuss like this, you're always such a brave girl.'

'No, don't go. I don't need the nurse. It doesn't hurt much, really. Oh Mum, I've broken my glasses! I'm *ever* so sorry.'

Mum didn't mind a bit about my glasses, even though they'd cost a lot of money. 'We ought to be able to Superglue them OK,' she said. 'I wish we could fix your poor old arm as easily! I'm sure it's broken.'

It turned out it wasn't broken at all. I just had a bad sprain, so they bandaged it up and put it in a sling.

'There. All done,' said the nurse, folding up the ends of the sling neatly. 'Don't jump under any more buses, young Mandy.'

I smiled politely but Mum looked fierce.

'She didn't jump, she was pushed,' said Mum.

The nurse wasn't paying proper attention as she rolled bandages. She smiled as if Mum were joking.

'It's not funny,' Mum burst out. 'It's a very serious matter. She could easily have been killed!'

'Mum!' I hissed. She sounded really cross. I'd never heard her be so rude to anyone before.

She put her arm round me to help me, and yet her own arm was shaking.

'Come along, Mandy,' she said, and she whisked me out of the cubicle and down the corridor so fast our shoes squeaked on the polished floor.

There was a bus stop right outside the hospital but Mum got us a taxi instead. I could only remember going in a taxi a couple of times before. If I wasn't so worried I'd have enjoyed sitting back pretending to be posh.

'The little girl been in the wars, has she?' said the taxi driver. 'Kids! When our two were that age we were forever up in the casualty. They keep you hanging around forever, don't they?'

'And when I got there I found my daughter all on her own,' Mum said furiously.

'I had a nurse talk to me before, Mum. I didn't mind,' I said.

'And they didn't even think it sensible to keep her in overnight in case of concussion,' said Mum.

'But the doctor looked in my eyes and checked me all over,' I said.

'Well, as soon as we get home I'm calling out Dr Mansfield and we'll see what he thinks,' said Mum.

She made me go to bed when I got in, though I kept insisting I was perfectly all right. She had to help me get undressed because it was so awkward managing with my arm in a sling – and it was my right arm too, which made me much clumsier trying to manage with my left.

Mum fixed me a special sick-bed tea, on her best black tray patterned with orangey-red poppies. The food was orange too: orange yolk in my boiled egg, orange satsumas, orange shreds in her home-made carrot cake and orange juice to drink.

I scrabbled under my pillow for Olivia Orang-utan. I collect monkeys. I've got twenty-two now. Some are really old and were Mummy's monkeys when she was a little girl. There's a huge great gorilla almost as big as me that Daddy gave me last Christmas. I like them all, but my favourite is Olivia. She's only as big as my hand and she's very soft and very hairy and very orange.

I tucked her in beside me and fed her some of my orange treat tea. When we were both finished I gave her a little ride in my sling.

'Mind your arm!' said Mum. 'That sling is so you can *rest* it. Don't jiggle it around like that.' She sat down on the side of my bed, looking very serious. 'Now, sweetheart. I want you to tell me exactly what happened.'

My heart started pounding under my

nightie. I clutched Olivia with my good hand. I looked down at the empty dishes on the poppy tray.

'You know what happened, Mum. I ran out in the road. And the bus came. I'm sorry, I know I should have looked first. I won't ever do it again, I swear I won't. Don't be cross.'

'I'm not cross with you, Mandy,' said Mum. 'Now, tell me *why* you ran out into the road.'

But the doorbell went, distracting us. It was Dr Mansfield, who'd just finished his evening surgery. He was nice at first and he admired Olivia and all my other monkeys, and he complimented my bandage and sling too, saying Mum had done a very professional job.

'The nurse at the hospital did it,' I said, and then Dr Mansfield got very irritated with Mum, saying that there was really no point in him examining me if I'd already been treated at the hospital.

I got all knotted up inside while they argued. I slid further and further under the covers, wishing I could snuggle right underneath and play caves with my monkey collection. I didn't want to resurface even after Dr Mansfield went because I knew Mum was going to start asking questions again and I didn't know what to say. So I pretended to be sleepy and said I wanted to have a little nap.

Mum usually thought little naps a good idea

but now she started feeling my forehead and asking if my head was hurting. I sussed that you feel sleepy if you get concussion. I started to worry whether I did have it after all, because I really was starting to get a pain in my head. I got scared and Mum got scared too, though she kept telling me that I'd be fine and I mustn't worry.

Then we heard the car outside and it was Dad back from London. He came running up the stairs when he heard the tone of Mum's voice. He never looks quite like Daddy when he's in his stripy office suit. He always has a shower and changes into his fisherman's smock and baggy old trousers the minute he gets in, and it's as if he's screwed on a new happy-old-Dad face too. But now he forgot all about changing. He sat on my bed while Mum said all this stuff. She started calmly but her voice got higher and higher and when she told how she came back from the dentists to find a woman waiting on her doorstep to tell her I'd been in an accident, she burst into tears.

'Don't, Mum!' I said, starting to cry too. 'I'm sorry. But I'm really all right now, I think my headache's just an ordinary one, and my wrist doesn't hurt at all, so don't cry, *please*.'

Dad put his arms round both of us until we'd both quietened down. Mum went off to make us all a cup of tea, still sniffling. Dad gave me an extra cuddle.

'Just so long as you're safe and sound, poppet. Don't worry about Mum. She's having a bit of bother with her nerves just now, and she's having to have all this horrid root canal work, and now you bump into a bus, old girl! Poor Mum. Poor Mandy.'

He made Olivia wipe my eyes with her soft paws and I was laughing by the time Mum came back to my room with the teatray. I hoped it was all sorted out. But then Mum started on about what the woman had told her, all this stuff about me being chased by these girls, and Dad sat up straight, and I knew there wasn't going to be any more laughing.

'Which girls chased you, Mandy?' said Dad.

'It's those three again, isn't it?' said Mum. 'Melanie and that really nasty big girl and the showy little girl with the curls. I can't understand how Melanie can be so horrid, she seemed such a nice girl, and I really got on well with her mother. I'm going to phone her up and—'

'No! No, you mustn't!' I said.

'Of course we've got to have this out,' said Mum. 'Their mothers need to be told. I should have tackled this right from the start when they turned on you. And we'll have to go to the school too and tell your teacher—'

'*No!* You can't!' I said desperately.

'Now, now, calm down, Mandy. Hey, you're spilling all your tea. Why are you getting in such a state? Have these girls really threatened you? Have they made you keep it all a secret? Are you really scared of them?' Dad asked.

'Of *course* she's scared, the poor little thing. So scared she ran right into the road. Oh dear, when I *think* what could have happened! She could have gone right under the bus and—' Mum was getting tearful again.

'Mandy, you've got to tell us exactly what these girls did,' said Dad.

'They didn't do anything!' I said frantically. 'I wish you wouldn't keep going on about it. And you mustn't tell their mums or anyone at school or else—'

'Or else what, pet?' said Dad.

'They'll all hate me,' I wailed.

'Don't be silly, Mandy, how could anyone ever hate you?' said Mum. 'You're a lovely girl. All your teachers always say you're a pleasure to have in their class. I suppose those girls are just jealous because you always come top and

28

you're obviously well loved and cared for. I know Melanie's mother was very worried that her divorce had badly unsettled Melanie. But still, that's no excuse for bullying, chasing you right out into the road.'

'It *wasn't* Melanie, it was Kim—' I sobbed.

'Ah. Which one is she?' said Dad.

'That big girl – the one who looks much older than her age. I've always thought her a nasty piece of work. I've heard her say some silly things behind *my* back,' said Mum. 'So what was she saying to you this afternoon, Mandy?'

'I – I can't remember.'

'Now then, sweetheart, it's quite important that you try,' said Dad. 'We've really got to get to the bottom of this, even though it's upsetting. She does frighten you, this Kim, doesn't she? Does she ever hit you?'

'No!'

'Are you sure, Mandy? She's so much bigger

than you. And when she was chasing you, are you *certain* she didn't push you?'

'No, she didn't, I swear she didn't,' I said. 'Look, please, I don't want to talk about it.'

I had Mum on one side of me, Dad the other. I felt smothered between them, and there was no getting away, no stopping their questions.

'I know it's upsetting for you, pet, but we've got to know,' said Dad. '*Why* were you running from them?'

'I just – I just wanted to get home.'

'But what were they saying?' said Mum.

'I *said*, I don't remember!' I shouted.

'Mandy?' They were both looking at me, so serious, so sorrowful.

'Come along, Mandy, we've never had any secrets in our family,' said Mum.

'You can tell us anything,' said Dad.

But I couldn't tell.

'I really truly don't remember,' I insisted. 'It's making my head hurt just thinking about it. Please can't I just go to sleep? *Please?*'

So they had to give in. I lay there in my bedroom after they'd tiptoed downstairs. It wasn't anywhere near dark. It wasn't my proper bedtime yet. I wasn't the slightest bit sleepy. I couldn't stop thinking about Kim and Sarah and Melanie. I wished I wasn't Mandy White. I started pretending. OK, I wasn't boring, baby, goody-goody Mandy White any more. I was . . . Miranda Rainbow. I was cool. I was colourful. I wore loads of make-up and had this ultra hip hairstyle. I wore the most amazing super sexy clothes. I had pierced ears and a stud in my nose. I didn't have a mum. I didn't have a dad. I lived all by myself in this incredible modern flat. Sometimes my friends stayed overnight at my place. I had heaps of friends and they all begged me to be their *best* friend.

I fell asleep being Miranda Rainbow but then Mum woke me up tucking the covers over me and I couldn't get back to sleep for ages. I couldn't stop myself being Mandy White in the middle of the night. I tossed and turned as the quarter-hours chimed, thinking about going to school tomorrow. Thinking about Melanie and Sarah. And Kim . . .

Mum brought me breakfast in bed on the poppy tray. She felt my forehead and looked at my face.

'You still look very peaky and you've got dark circles under your eyes. I think you'd be better off having a quiet day in bed, just to be on the safe side,' said Mum.

For once I was so so glad that my mum was

such a worrier and always fussing. I didn't have to face Kim and Melanie and Sarah. I could stay at home. Safe.

Mum phoned up her work and pretended she was sick.

'It's not really a fib, Mandy,' she said uncomfortably. 'My teeth are still playing up.'

'But you could have gone to work, Mum. I'd be fine by myself,' I said.

'I'd much sooner stay home with you, darling,' said Mum.

Mum didn't like her work much now anyway. She was a company director's secretary, but her company had changed its director and this new one was young and Mum didn't think much of him. She job-shared with another lady, and Mum didn't think much of the afternoon secretary either. She was young, too.

She got in a bit of a state telling me all about them and I got bored, but tried to nod in all the right places. Then Mum tried hard to play with me, but that got a bit boring too. I was glad when she went downstairs to get started on lunch. I tried doing some colouring with my felt-tips but my wrist hurt too much. I got so fed up I tipped the tin up. There were rainbow felt-tips scattered all over the carpet. I got out of bed, sighing, and started picking them all up. Several had rolled right over to the window. I wandered over and stared out, not really

focusing through my glued-together glasses.
Someone was rocking the pram in the garden
over the road.

There were always babies over there. Mrs
Williams was a foster mother. But the person
at the pram certainly wasn't Mrs Williams.
She's big and she wears old Indian clothes. This
person was small and startling. I thought she
was a grown-up at first. She was wearing very
short shorts and a top that showed her tummy,
and great clacky high heels. But when I
screwed up my eyes to have a proper stare I saw
her face wasn't really that old, though she was
wearing lots of make-up. She had short sticky-
up hair, bright orange, the exact colour of
Olivia Orang-utan's fur.

She looked up and saw me staring at her at
the window. She crossed her eyes and stuck her
tongue out, and then she waved at me. As if we
knew each other.

YELLOW

Yellow

There was a phone call for me at teatime.

'A boy!' Mum mouthed, handing the phone over.

I stared at the phone as if it was a wild animal. There was a voice saying something. I held the receiver very gingerly to my ear.

'. . . so they didn't keep you in hospital long, Mandy? Have you broken anything? Remember when I broke my leg last year and I had that great plaster cast and everyone wrote stuff all over it, even poems, remember that rude one?'

It was only Arthur King. I wasn't really nervous of him.

'I've hurt my wrist, but it's not broken, it's just got a sling. You can't write on it because it's only material.'

'Oh, well. Never mind. I mean, I'm ever so glad you're all right.'

'Mmmm.'

'You're *sure* you're all right? You haven't got concussion, have you? You're not saying very much.'

'You're not giving me a chance,' I said.

Arthur King gave his funny daft-dog laugh, yaaa-yaaa-yaaa, but he still sounded anxious.

'Mandy?'

'Yes?'

'Mmm. Mandy?' he repeated, suddenly tongue-tied.

'What?'

'I feel bad about yesterday. I just stood there. When they were saying all that stuff.'

'Well, they weren't saying it about you.'

'Yes, but I should have rescued you.'

'You what?' I said, snorting with laughter. Arthur King is smaller than me and he's always left till last when people pick teams for Games.

'It wasn't very chivalrous,' said Arthur.

'You what?' I repeated.

'Mandy, don't keep using that horrible uncouth expression,' Mum hissed in the background. 'Who *is* this boy?'

'Arthur's in my class at school,' I said.

'I know I'm in your class at

school,' said Arthur. 'Mandy, I think you *have* got concussion.'

'No, I was just telling my mum who you are, that's all,' I said.

'Your tea's getting cold, Mandy,' said Mum. 'Come along, dear. Say bye bye.'

'I've got to go in a minute, Arthur,' I said. 'Shiver-what?'

'What's that?'

'You said you weren't shivering or something. Yesterday.'

'Chivalrous! Like a knight. Like my name-sake, King Arthur. I didn't rescue the damsel in distress, did I? I just stood there and I *was* shivering. Scared. Cowardy custard. Yellow. That was me.'

'It's OK, Arthur. Really. Anyway I'm cowardly, too.'

'Yes, but it's all right for you, because you're a girl.'

'Look, we're not back in those days of all the knights. Girls aren't supposed to be rescued now. They're meant to sort themselves out.'

'But there were three of them and only one of you. I'm a rotten coward. And I'm sorry. Ever so sorry, Mandy.'

'That's quite all right, Arthur,' I said politely. 'I have to get on with my tea now. Bye.'

I felt pleased that Arthur had phoned me. I'd never ever had a boy phone me up before. It felt good. *I* felt good.

But the next morning I insisted I felt really bad.

'I don't feel at all well, Mum,' I said. 'And my wrist *aches*.'

'Oh, darling.' Mum looked at me anxiously. Dad had already left for his work. She didn't have anyone to consult.

'*Please* can I stay at home?'

Mum felt my forehead and looked at me carefully.

'I don't think you've got a temperature. But you do still look a bit peaky. And I don't suppose there's really much point going to school if you can't write properly. All right, then. As it's Friday anyway. But you really will have to go back to school on Monday, Mandy.'

Monday seemed quite a long way away. I could try to forget about it for the moment.

I begged Mum to go back to work. I promised her I'd be fine by myself. I said I'd even stay in bed so she'd know I was absolutely safe. But she wouldn't hear of it. She phoned in sick again.

'Aren't we bad girls?' said Mum. 'Shall we do some baking together, hm? Give Daddy a surprise when he comes home from work. I'll do an iced sponge – chocolate or coffee? You choose, pet. And some fairy cakes? And then how

38

about some gingerbread men?'

I couldn't help much with the sifting and stir-
ring – but my left hand managed the
bowl-licking perfectly.

When the cakes and biscuits were all baking,
filling the house with warm sweet smells, I left
Mum to do the washing up and went upstairs
to my bedroom to fetch a book. I peered over at
Mrs Williams' house. The pram was in the
garden and I could see the baby on its back
waving its legs in the air. But there was no sign
of the girl with orange hair.

I kept popping back to my bedroom during
the morning. The baby was crying one time,
but Mrs Williams came out to see to it. She
didn't bother rocking it, she just wheeled it
indoors. But then just before lunch I saw her!
The girl. She was walking down the road
towards the house carrying two shopping bags.
She was wearing her clacky high heels again,
so it was quite hard for her to balance. She was
in leggings today and a T-shirt with a man's
face. I guessed he was a rock star.

She had a Walkman on and was bobbing her
orange head in time to the music in her ears.
She even did one or two funny little dance steps
in spite of her shoes and the shopping. I smiled
– and she suddenly looked up and saw me.

I bobbed back behind the curtain, my heart
thudding. I heard the squeak of the Williams'

gate and a clack clack clack. I peeped round the curtain. She was still craning up at me. When she saw me looking she waved again. I waved back though I tried to wave my arm in the sling first and then changed to my good arm, feeling silly and clumsy. She started mouthing something. I thought she was singing along to her music, but she was looking straight at me.

I squinted behind my glasses, trying to read her lips. It was no use. I shook my head hopelessly. She dumped the shopping on the path and made opening and pushing gestures. I didn't even get that for a minute, and then I realized. She wanted me to open the window. But I couldn't open the big windows because they were fitted with special locks, so I had to shake my head again.

She sighed with exasperation, her eyebrows raised, and then she picked up her bags and banged on the door with her elbow. She was so skinny I was surprised it didn't hurt.

I spent half the afternoon staring out the window, hoping she might come out again.

'Do stop mooning about, Mandy,' said Mum. 'I've made a nice cup of tea – and we'll try a fairy cake, eh? Come on, cheer up.'

Mum lifted my plaits up either side of my head and pulled. I was supposed to smile.

I shook my head free.

'Mum, can I have my hair cut?'

'Oh, darling, don't be silly. Your hair's lovely.'

'No, it's not. I've got sick of it long. And I don't want plaits any more, *no-one* has plaits nowadays, it just looks stupid. Can't I have my hair short – and sort of sticking up?'

'Like a bird's nest!' said Mum, munching fairy cake.

'Mum, has Mrs Williams got any daughters? Real ones, I mean, not the foster babies.' I started licking the icing off the top of my fairy cake.

'Don't eat it like that, pet. Yes, I think she's got one grown-up daughter in Canada.'

'This girl isn't grown-up.'

'Which girl?'

'At the Williams' house. I saw her yesterday. And today. She was helping with one of the babies and doing the shopping.'

'Maybe she's a granddaughter then. About your age?'

'Older.'

'Still, it would be nice if you had someone to make friends with. Now that Melanie's turned so silly.'

I shivered, wanting to keep the whole scary school world separate.

'Tell you what, Mandy! How about taking some of these cakes over to Mrs Williams? There's far too many for us. And it'll give you the chance to get to know this girl.'

'No, Mum! No. I don't want to,' I said, suddenly desperately shy.

'Don't be so soppy,' said Mum, arranging the cakes carefully in one of her Tupperware boxes. 'There! Over you go.'

'No, Mum. Please. I'd feel stupid,' I said.

I desperately wanted to get to know the girl and yet I really couldn't just march over and knock on their door. She'd smiled and waved, and yet she'd pulled the face too. She looked as if she could be really really tough if she wanted. Even tougher than Kim.

'You are a funny little poppet,' Mum said fondly. 'Shall I come with you?'

'I don't want to go at all,' I said, and I wouldn't budge.

So Mum went over to see Mrs Williams by herself. I waited in the kitchen, making a pattern in the cake-crumbs. Mum was gone quite a long time. I wished I'd had the courage to go over by myself. Miranda Rainbow would have rushed over the road without a second thought. Why did I always have to be such a silly coward? Cowardy cowardy custard. That was something they called me at school. And Baby. And Polly Pigtails. And Four-Eyes. And Snobby-Swot. Kim invented new names, new games almost every day.

What would she do to me on Monday?

I crammed another fairy cake in my mouth even though I was starting to feel sick. Then I heard the front door. Mum was back, looking a little pink.

'Oh dear, oh dear, that was a bit awkward,' she said. 'Mandy! You silly girl, you didn't tell me what this Tanya was *like*.'

Tanya! A lovely exotic, unusual name. As good as Miranda. No, *better*. It really suited her.

'Tanya,' I said dreamily.

'Do you know, she calls Mrs Williams "Pat" – not even *Aunty* Pat. Though of course she's not related,' said Mum. 'She's a foster child. There was some trouble at the last home she was in. She's meant to be very good with little children so Mrs Williams said she'd take her on for a few weeks. She says she's quite a helpful little thing, considering. But whatever does she *look* like!'

'I think she looks lovely,' I said.

'Oh, Mandy,' said Mum, and she laughed at

43

me. 'Still, she seemed quite smitten with you too, asking all about you. And she wanted to ask you over to play, but I said you still weren't very well after a nasty accident, and you were having a little lie down.'

'*Mum!*'

'But you said you didn't want to go over there. You insisted!'

'Yes, but – if she *wants* me to . . .'

'Well, I'd really much sooner you didn't. A girl like that! You haven't got anything in common. And she's much older than you anyway. I thought she'd be at least sixteen but she's only just fourteen, can you credit it? The heels she was wearing! I hope Mrs Williams knows what she's taking on.' Mum clucked her teeth.

I crumbled the rest of my fairy cake, wishing and wishing I'd gone over to the Williams' house myself. Tanya would think me a hopeless baby now, after the way Mum had talked about me. I *was* a hopeless baby. Tanya would never really want to make friends with me.

But less than an hour later there was a knock on the door. A jaunty rat-tatta-ta-tat-*tat*.

'I wonder who that is?' said Mum, getting up. I knew!

'Hiya!' said Tanya, as soon as Mum got the door open. She licked her lips as if she was chasing crumbs. 'Thanks for the little cakes, they were smashing.' She held out the empty plate.

'You haven't eaten them all?' said Mum, startled.

'You bet I have,' said Tanya. 'Well, Simon and Charlie licked the icing off a couple. The baby can't eat cakes because it hasn't got any teeth yet, and poor old Pat is trying to stick to this dopey old diet. So I got lucky, didn't I?' She patted her completely flat stomach and winked. She wasn't looking at Mum now. She was looking past her, at me.

'You're Mandy, right?' she said.

I nodded.

'Let's have a chat, then,' said Tanya, and she marched into the hall in her high heels, neatly dodging Mum's big hip.

Mum turned round, frowning.

'Well, I really think Mandy ought to have a bit of a rest just now,' she said, in her bossiest voice. 'Perhaps another time.' When she uses that voice to me my stomach always squeezes and I do as I'm told.

Tanya just laughed. Not rudely. She had this

beautiful sunny laugh that made you want to smile too. Even Mum.

'But she's *had* a rest, haven't you, Mandy? You want me to come and play with you, don't you?'

She was talking to me as if I was much younger, one of Mrs Williams' toddlers. I didn't care.

I nodded, still unable to say a word.

Tanya was right down the hall beside me now. She put out her hand and touched my arm. She wore purple nail varnish though her nails were bitten right down so that the ends of her fingers bulged. But somehow even they looked glamorous.

'Show us your bedroom, then,' said Tanya, giving me a little push.

I started up the stairs obediently, Tanya following, tapping out a tune on the bannister with her nibbled nails. Mum was left in the hall, the front door still open though it was obvious Tanya was staying.

'Well, just for ten minutes, then,' said Mum reluctantly.

She still hovered uneasily. I was terrified she might come up too. I deliberately didn't look back at her, and when Tanya and I were in my bedroom I shut the door.

'Wow!' said Tanya looking round.

I blinked at her. It sounded as if she actually

liked my room. Melanie had always been very dismissive.

'It's all pink and pretty and girlie,' said Tanya, kicking off her heels and jumping onto my white fluffy rug. She wiggled her toes. 'I've always wanted one of these rugs. How do you keep it so clean, eh? Oh, and I like your *bed*!'

She took a running dive at it, bouncing happily on the pink sprigged duvet, then lying right down, her hair bright on my frilly pillow. 'Mmm, it smells so clean too,' she said, picking the pillow up and sniffing it appreciatively. She dislodged Olivia.

'Hello? Who's this, then?'

I swallowed. 'I have this monkey collection,' I said hoarsely, waving in the direction of the monkey shelf. They were all neatly arranged, paws folded, tails twirling down from the shelf in little loops, apart from Gertrude Gorilla who didn't have a tail and was far too big to sit on the shelf anyway. She sat beside it, her arms out as if she were saying how much she loved me.

Tanya hurtled straight off the bed into Gertrude's hairy arms, using her as an arm-chair.

'He tickles,' said Tanya.

I decided not to bother explaining that Gertrude was a she. I was getting giddy watching Tanya whizzing round and round my room. I sat shyly on the edge of my bed as if I were the guest.

Tanya still had hold of Olivia.

'This one's still my favourite,' she said.

'She's mine too,' I said, pleased. 'Her name's Olivia.' I blushed, scared Tanya would think me stupid giving my monkeys names.

'Hello, Olivia. Haven't you got a posh name?' said Tanya. She made Olivia's head waggle. 'Oooh yes, I should jolly well say so,' she said, pretending to be Olivia. She had her voice all wrong, but it didn't really matter.

'She's got the same colour hair as me!' said Tanya, and she screwed up her face into a funny monkey expression to match. 'Do you like it this colour, eh, Mandy?'

'I think it's lovely,' I said.

'Of course, it's not *really* this colour. It's sort of mouse naturally. Only that's boring, isn't it?'

'Oh, yes.'

'I thought I might try it black some time. Go all Gothic and witchy. What do you think?'

I didn't know what to say. I was amazed she was asking my opinion. I still couldn't believe she was actually in my bedroom, chatting away to me.

'Or I could go blonde, like you,' said Tanya 'You've got lovely hair.'

'Me?' I said, astonished.

'My little sister's got long hair too. Just like yours. You look like her. I thought just for a minute you were her when I saw you up at the window. Mad, eh?'

I smiled nervously.

'I used to do our Carmel's hair every day. I'm good at long hair. I'll style yours for you, if you like.'

'*Would* you?'

'Sure,' said Tanya.

She sat me down in front of my dressing table and undid my stupid plaits. She brushed out my hair really carefully, not pulling anywhere near as much as Mum does.

'I'm ever so gentle, aren't I?' said Tanya. 'That's because Carmel yells her head off if you tug her tangles. And she wiggles around some-

49

thing awful. You're *much* better behaved than Carmel.'

'Is Carmel at Mrs Williams' too?' I asked.

Tanya stood still. Her face screwed up. I got scared. She went on brushing my hair after a moment, but she didn't answer. I didn't dare try asking her again.

She swept my hair up and wound it round her fingers and then with one deft twiddle turned it into a top knot. She secured it with the bands from my plaits.

'Like it?'

'Oh, wow!' I said.

'And we'll soften it up here at the front,' said Tanya, pulling a wisp over my forehead and doing little curly bits in front of my ears. 'Yeah?'

'Yeah!' I said, trying to say it just the way she did.

I looked so different. Grown up. Almost Miranda Rainbow.

'Got any spray?' said Tanya.

I shook my head.

'You need it, to keep it in place. And you can get all sorts of special slides and bands if you want to wear it up. Carmel used to have heaps.'

Tanya paused. 'I did my little brothers' hair too, cut it once a month and everything. I kept

them looking really nice. I've got two little brothers, Sean and Matty. And my Carmel. I looked after them just like I was their mum. That's why they're trying me out at Pat's place. Because I'm good with little kids. But I hoped she'd have girls. Huh! Pat's got little Simon and that gormless Charlie and baby Ricky and they *all* yell and muck around and get messy and play with their willies. I'm sick of little boys. *And* big boys. Me and my boyfriend broke up three weeks ago, and do you know something, it's the best thing that's ever happened to me, because he is a pig.'

She didn't just say he was a pig. She swore and I felt my cheeks go red and I hoped she wouldn't notice. I was ever so glad I'd shut the bedroom door so Mum couldn't hear.

'Yeah, all boys give me the creeps,' Tanya insisted. 'So that's why I thought I'd find a little girl to play with.' She smiled at me kindly. I smiled back, but I couldn't help fidgeting.

'I'm not actually a *little* girl,' I said. 'I'm ten.'

Tanya blinked at me. 'You're never! I thought you were only about eight. Aren't you tiny!'

I blushed even more.

'Still, I'm tiny too. Without my heels,' said Tanya. She saw me looking at them admiringly. 'You can try them on if you want.'

'*Can* I?' I kicked off my slippers and edged my

feet inside the black suede straps. They looked *wonderful*.

The bedroom door suddenly opened and I fell off one shoe in shock.

'Mandy! Watch your ankles,' said Mum, coming in with a tray. She frowned. 'It's not very nice to try on other people's shoes,' she said.

I took the other high heel off, sighing. 'Whatever have you done with your hair?' said Mum.

'Tanya did it. I think it looks fantastic,' I said.

'Hm,' said Mum putting the tray on my bedside table. She looked at Tanya. 'I thought you might like a drink and a snack. Before you go home,' she said. 'Though you'll still be full up with cake.'

'Ooh, no, I'm always starving – even though I stay so skinny,' said Tanya. 'Is that Coke?'

'No, it's Ribena actually,' said Mum. 'And some gingerbread men. Home-made.'

'Gingerbread *folk*,' said Tanya. 'We made them at this home I was in, and it was sexist to call them men, because women wear trousers too, don't they?' She picked up a gingerbread person, examining it carefully. 'We'll make this one definitely a woman, eh, Mandy?' She

52

nibbled along the stumpy legs with her sharp little teeth. 'There, she's wearing leggings now!' Tanya laughed and I laughed too. I took a gingerbread person even though I was far too excited to be hungry. I nibbled as well.

'There, I've got a woman too,' I said, spraying crumbs.

'Don't talk with your mouth full, Mandy,' said Mum. She walked over to my bed, tidying the duvet and pillow. She looked like she might be intending to sit on it herself.

'You can go now, Mum,' I blurted out quickly.

Mum looked surprised and hurt, but she didn't say anything.

She went. My heart started thudding in case I'd hurt her feelings but I couldn't bother about it too much. Not now. With Tanya.

She slurped her Ribena. 'New lipstick, eh, Mandy?' she said, smacking stained lips. 'It'll match my nails a treat.'

She ate her gingerbread woman, and pretended to feed Olivia and Gertrude too, kidding around as if she still thought me a baby. But it didn't matter. Nothing mattered in the whole world because I was friends with Tanya.

She pretended to feed the man's face on her T-shirt too.

'Here, Kurt, you can have a mouthful,' she said.

'Who?'

'You don't know who *Kurt* is?'
Tanya rolled her eyes and sighed.
She reverently stroked his tousled
fringe. 'Only the greatest rock
star ever, and I just love him.'
   'I thought you said all boys
gave you the creeps?' I said
boldly.
   She gave me a little nudge.
'You're not so shy now, are you?
And anyway, Miss Clever-Clogs,
he's not a boy.'
   'Well, a man, then.'
   'He's not a man either. He's an angel,
because he's dead. Or a devil.'
   'He's dead?' I said, surprised, because he
looked so young.
   'He committed suicide,' said Tanya. She got
up off Gertrude and wandered round my room,
opening the drawers in my play cupboard.
   I didn't mind her fiddling with my things at
all. She got out my big tin of rainbow felt-tips.
   'Wow! Do they all work still?'
   'Yes.'
   'Let's draw, eh? I *love* colouring.'
   I found us both some drawing paper. I took
my arm out of my sling and waggled my fingers.
Yes, I thought I could draw OK. My wrist hurt
but I didn't care. I usually drew at my desk, but
Tanya spread herself full-length on the carpet,

leaning her paper on one of my books. I did the same.

'My mum committed suicide,' said Tanya. She said it so casually I wasn't quite sure I'd heard her properly. I stared at her. Tanya saw I was shocked.

'She topped herself,' she said, thinking I didn't know what suicide meant.

'How . . . awful,' I mumbled.

'Well, she was always a bit zonked out of her brains anyway,' said Tanya. 'It's OK, it was ages and ages ago. I was quite little. Though I can still remember her. I'll draw her, shall I?'

She drew a lovely lady in a long purple dress and she gave her purple wings too, with rows of jade and aqua feathers like frills.

I didn't know what to draw. I didn't want to draw my mum.

'Draw me,' said Tanya.

So I drew her as carefully as

I could, trying very hard to make her pretty. I did her short orange hair and her smiley mouth and her little purple nails. I did every strap on her shoes. I even did a portrait of her Kurt on her T-shirt.

'That's good,' said Tanya. 'OK, I'll draw you now.'

She drew a funny, podgy, little girl with lots of long yellow hair. I wasn't sure whether I was pleased or not. She saw me hesitating, so she drew me special strappy high-heeled clunky sandals on my feet. She did a long line of green grass under me. The heels on my shoes didn't quite touch it, so I looked as if I was doing a little dance. She drew a blue line of sky at the top of the page, and then right above my head she did a big yellow sun with rays all round it.

Then she wrote a title at the top. Her writing was rather wobbly and I knew she'd spelled a word wrong but it didn't matter a bit.

MY FREND MANDY. That's what she wrote. And I felt so happy I felt as if there was a real sun above my head and I was dancing in its warm yellow rays.

MY FREND MANDY

GREEN

Green

I had to go to school on Monday. Mum took me. She wore her best navy suit though it's really too small for her now. It's got tiny lines called pinstripes. Mum had pinstripes across her forehead too. She only frowns like that when she's very cross.

'Oh, Mum, please, promise you won't say anything,' I begged.

I nearly died when we turned the corner and caught up Melanie and her mother. Melanie went bright red when she saw me. She looked as if she was going to cry.

Melanie's mum started talking to my mum about the weather and the holidays and grown-up stuff like that. Melanie and I shuffled along trying not to look at each other. Then I heard Melanie give a little sniff.

'I thought you might be dead,' she whispered.

I blinked at her.

'When you didn't come to school the next day. And Arthur saïd you were taken off in the ambulance. But you're all right now?'

'It's just my wrist.' I held my arm out though there was nothing to show. I didn't need the sling any more.

'Oh, Mandy.' Melanie blew upwards with relief, ruffling her fluffy fringe. 'Even Kim was in a right state, I can tell you.'

I giggled nervously.

'Mandy . . .' Melanie struggled. 'Well, I'm glad you're all right.'

I nodded, knowing there were lots of things she wanted to say but couldn't. I felt as if a huge breath was ruffling me all over, making me light and bouncy. I was all right. Melanie was

59

glad I was all right. It looked as if *everything* was going to be all right again now.

But as we got nearer school Melanie stepped aside from me and went quiet. I realized it was in case Kim saw us. And then at the school gate Mum suddenly stopped speaking to Melanie's mum and looked hard at Melanie.

'It's a shame you're not Mandy's friend any more,' said Mum.

Melanie went red again. Melanie's mum looked embarrassed too.

'Yes, I don't know why they've had their little tiff. Still, girls will be girls,' she said uneasily.

'It's more than a little tiff,' said Mum. 'I don't really blame your Melanie. It's that other girl. Kim.'

'Yes, I don't know why Melanie's got so pally with her. I don't see why they can't *all* be friends anyway. But I expect they'll sort it out between themselves,' said Melanie's mum.

'I'm going to make sure things are sorted out,' said Mum, and she marched through the school gate and into the playground.

I dashed after her.

'Mum! Mum, where are you going? What are you doing?'

'I'm going to have a little word with Mrs Edwards,' said Mum.

I felt faint. The headmistress.

'Mum, you *can't* tell Mrs Edwards,' I said, my

voice squeaking with shock. 'They'll all hate me and think I'm a sneaky tell-tale.'

'Don't be silly, darling,' said Mum. 'And you needn't get at all involved. You can go off to your classroom and forget all about it. I just need to let Mrs Edwards know what's happening in her school.'

'But you don't understand, you *can't* . . .' I wailed.

She could. I had no way of stopping her.

I trailed into Mrs Stanley's classroom. Kim was there, standing at the front. She seemed to grow. I seemed to shrink. Melanie was yacking away to her, pointing at me. Sarah was there too, chewing her lip as she listened. I heard the word Mandy. I heard the word Mum.

'Right,' said Kim, and she put her hands on her hips and turned to me.

But Mrs Stanley came bustling in with a basket of roses and started cheerily chatting about her weekend in the country. She sent me off to fill some vases with water for the flowers. I wished there was some way I could stay in the cloakroom all day long, filling vase after vase for a whole field of flowers. But I had to go back and arrange the roses and answer the register and then get out my things for Maths when all the time I was peering out the window to see if Mum had finished seeing Mrs Edwards.

It was halfway through the lesson when I

spotted Mum going across the playground, looking hot and uncomfortable in her tight suit. Her skirt rode up and showed her fat knees. The tightness of her skirt made her walk with a waggle. I saw Kim wiggling her shoulders imitating Mum. Someone giggled.

I bent over my Maths book and pretended to be working, though all the numbers squirmed across the page and my hands were so wet that I smudged the sums I'd already done.

I hoped that it was all over now. But it wasn't all over. It was just beginning.

One of Mrs Edwards' monitors suddenly came into our classroom.

'Excuse me, Mrs Stanley, but Mrs Edwards wants to see Kim Matthews, Melanie Holder and Sarah Newman in her office straight away.' The monitor announced this importantly, so that everyone heard.

All heads swivelled towards Kim and Melanie and Sarah. Sarah started chewing her lip so violently that her mouth went sideways.

Melanie looked like ice cream, white and wet. But Kim looked perfectly composed, though her cheeks were a little pinker than usual. And her eyes brighter. As she looked at me.

I knew what her look meant.

She was really really really going to get me now.

I bent right over my Maths book, clenching everything. I stayed like that long after they'd left the classroom.

I suddenly felt a hand on my shoulder and jumped.

'What's the matter, Mandy?' said Mrs Stanley.

I shook my head, trying to pretend.

'Why are you sitting like that, dear? Have you got a tummyache?'

I nodded.

Mrs Stanley bent closer. 'Do you need to go to the toilet?'

I nodded again.

'Well, why didn't you say so, you silly girl?' said Mrs Stanley. 'Really. You're not a baby, Mandy. Off you go, then.'

I shot off and sat in the dank toilets, crying, wishing I *was* a baby. A little helpless baby who didn't ever have to go to school. One of Mrs Williams' babies in a pram. And then Tanya could still come and play with me.

I sat in the toilets for ages. I read all the rude rhymes, much much ruder than anything Arthur had ever had written on his plaster cast. Then someone came into the toilets calling my name.

'Mandy White, are you in here?'

I hunched up small behind the door, hoping they'd go away.

There was a hammering on the door.

'Are you in there, Mandy? Because Mrs Stanley says if you're really not well you'd better go to the office, and you've got to go to the office *anyway* because Mrs Edwards wants you.'

It was no use. I couldn't stay silent behind the door forever. She'd jump up and look over the top in a minute.

'Just coming,' I mumbled, and flushed the toilet.

I came out and washed my hands. The monitor looked at me curiously.

'What were you *doing* in there?'

I shook my head, not answering.

'Were you sick?'

'No.' Though I was starting to *feel* sick. I looked at myself in the spotted mirror. I was a weird pale greeny colour. A lighter shade of the bottle green cardigan that Mum had knitted for me, even though everyone else had proper shop-bought jumpers.

'Come *on*, then.'

I followed her out of the toilets and along the corridors. I smelt the school dinners cooking in the canteen and felt sicker than ever. Kim and Sarah and Melanie were waiting outside Mrs Edwards' office. I wondered if I was going to throw up all over my carefully-fitted Clarks sandals.

Sarah and Melanie looked as if they felt sick too. Melanie was actually crying. But not Kim.

I didn't dare look at her properly as I scuttled past. I knocked on Mrs Edwards' door and stumbled in. I'd never ever been in her office before. You only got summoned if you'd been very naughty or cheeky or disruptive.

'Ah! Where have you been, Mandy? We've practically had to send out a search party,' said Mrs Edwards.

I hadn't often talked to her in all my years at the school. I'd shaken her hand at Prize Day, and once when I'd done the reading at Assembly she'd smiled at me and said 'Well Done'.

'I was . . .' I didn't like to say the word toilet to her. I just stood there, not finishing my sentence.

'Sit down, then, Mandy. Now. I hear you've been having a rather unhappy time at school recently?'

I sat down and stared hard at my lap. 'I . . . '
I didn't know what to say to this either.

'You've certainly done very well at your
lessons, and you've seemed happy and cheerful
enough as far as we could see,' said Mrs
Edwards briskly.

'Oh, yes,' I said, desperate to agree.

'But for a while now there have been some
girls who have been upsetting you?'

I bent lower.

'Some girls in your class?' Mrs Edwards persisted.

My head was nearly touching my clasped
hands.

'Mandy! Sit up straight. Now, there's no need
to look so worried. We're going to get this little
problem all sorted out. If you'd only told your

teacher about it earlier then it would have been so much easier to nip this nasty bullying in the bud. So, why don't you tell me all about it?' She waited.

I waited too. Mrs Edwards took her glasses off and rubbed the purple pinch marks on the bridge of her nose. She was trying to be patient.

'Now look, Mandy, there's no need to be frightened. You can tell me. I know it all already, but I just want to hear it from your lips.' She paused. She sighed. She put her glasses back on and peered at me. 'It's Kim and Sarah and Melanie, isn't it?' she said. 'So what have they been saying to you, mmm?'

I couldn't speak. I opened my mouth but no words came out. I couldn't gather together all those worrying weeks of teasing and squeeze them out into short sentences. Especially not with Kim and Sarah and Melanie waiting just the other side of the door.

'Your mother says they've been tormenting you, is that right?' Mrs Edwards persisted. 'And last Wednesday they chased you right out into the road and you were knocked down by a bus? Is that true, Mandy? Because this is very, very serious and it has to be dealt with. Did they chase you, Mandy? *Did* they?'

'Well. Sort of,' I mumbled into my lap.

'Aha!' said Mrs Edwards. 'So what were they saying to you?'

'I – I can't remember,' I said, shaking my head to stop the words echoing in my ears.

'Well, what sort of things do they usually say?' Mrs Edwards demanded.

'I forget,' I said.

Mrs Edwards sighed. She stood up. She suddenly went over to her door, swiftly in her stubby heels, and opened it up. Kim shot backwards, taken by surprise.

'So you've been listening, Kim!' said Mrs Edwards. 'Well, why don't you three girls come in here and join us? Perhaps we'll only start to get somewhere if we all talk this through together.'

They came crowding into the office. I shrank down into my chair. Mrs Edwards shut the door and sat on the edge of her desk frowning at Kim. Kim was taller than her. She had her head stuck in the air, one hand on her hip, acting like she couldn't care less. Melanie and Sarah were shuffling and drooping, much more scared.

'As doubtless you heard for yourself, Mandy here is being incredibly loyal to you girls, refusing to say anything against you,' said Mrs Edwards.

They all looked at me. Melanie blinked at me gratefully. Sarah sniffed.

'But it's obvious to me that you three girls have been very unkind to Mandy and this has got to stop, do you hear? I detest bullying. I won't have it in my school. Now, Kim, Melanie, Sarah, I want you three to say you're sorry to Mandy, and promise that you won't call her any nasty names or chase her ever again.'

They swallowed. Melanie started to say sorry. But Kim interrupted.

'I think Mandy should say sorry to us,' she said, tossing her head.

Even Mrs Edwards was taken aback.

'It was just as much Mandy's fault,' Kim went on smoothly. 'That's what started it. She told us these stories about her mum being a fashion model—'

Mrs Edwards' lips twitched. She was obviously thinking about Mum in her too-tight suit.

'Don't be ridiculous, Kim,' she said crisply. 'Don't make things worse for yourself telling these silly lies.'

'I'm not lying, Mrs Edwards,' said Kim. 'You *did* say that, didn't you, Mandy?'

I bent my head further. I knew I was going very red.

'Mandy?' said Mrs Edwards, her voice wavering.

'It was Mandy who told the lies, Mrs Edwards,' said Sarah.

'And then when we told her we knew she was lying she got really furious and she shouted at us and then she hit me,' said Kim.

'Now really, Kim, you can't expect me to believe that,' said Mrs Edwards. 'Mandy's half your size.'

'But she still hit me. Really hard.'

'She did, Mrs Edwards. She punched Kim straight in the face,' said Sarah.

'Yes, she did,' Melanie said, joining in. 'She hit Kim.'

'And then she ran away and she wasn't looking where she was going so she got hit by the bus,' said Kim. 'It was all *Mandy*, Mrs Edwards.'

Mrs Edwards got up and came and stood beside me. She put her arm round the back of the chair, and bent her head towards me so that her pepperminty breath tickled my cheek.

'You didn't hit Kim, did you, Mandy?' she said softly.

I shut my eyes.

'Just tell the truth, dear,' said Mrs Edwards.

'Yes, I hit her,' I said, and then I burst into tears.

Kim was triumphant. Mrs Edwards looked at me as if I'd let her down.

'I still can't quite believe it of you, Mandy,' she said. But then she frowned at Kim and the others. 'However, I know that you three have certainly been ganging up on Mandy recently. It's got to stop. You're not to call her names or say anything horrid to her, do you understand?'

'Oh yes, Mrs Edwards, we understand,' said Kim. 'We won't say *anything* to Mandy.'

That was the catch. She kept to her word. She didn't say anything at all to me. Neither did Sarah. Neither did Melanie. Kim marched them off and by lunchtime they had their act perfected. They hovered near me, but they didn't speak. They looked at me, they nudged each other, they made faces . . . but they didn't say anything.

I tried to pretend I was Miranda Rainbow, far too cool to care. It wouldn't work though, not with them bobbing about in the background.

Arthur King came over to me, his eyes twitching behind his glasses. He was holding a big old book and he offered it to me like a talisman.

'Here's that book I was telling you about, Mandy,' he said, gabbling a little. 'Do you want to have a look at it?'

Kim screeched with unkind laughter. Sarah and Melanie giggled.

'Over here. Where we can have a bit of peace,' said Arthur, steering me away from them.

The book was *King Arthur and the Knights of the Round Table*. I flipped through it gratefully, my hands shaking as I turned the pages.

Kim and Sarah and Melanie followed.

'Look, clear off,' said Arthur, trying to sound threatening.

'We've got a perfect right to be in this playground, same as you,' said Kim. 'We're not doing anything. And we're not saying anything to *her.*'

She thrust her chin at me, smacking her lips together to show they were sealed. Sarah and Melanie copied.

Mrs Stanley was on playground duty. She walked in our direction. She saw Kim and Sarah and Melanie. But I suppose they looked as if they were smiling at me.

'Let's get away from those loonies,' Arthur muttered, and he pulled me right over to the edge of the playground, by the boys' toilets. Where the girls never go.

We leaned against the wall and looked at Arthur's book together. Kim and Sarah and Melanie kept away, maybe because Mrs Stanley kept walking backwards and forwards across the playground keeping an eye on things.

Arthur kept finding me his favourite bits and reading paragraphs to me. It wasn't really my sort of thing at all. The king and the knights all spoke in this weird old-fashioned way, and I kept getting them all mixed up, but it didn't really matter. I did like the pictures, especially the women with their flowing hair and long swirly dresses. They looked a little like the picture Tanya had drawn of her mother.

My mother came to collect me from school. She wanted to know what Mrs Edwards had said to me, what she had done, how she had dealt with Kim and Melanie and Sarah.

'*Sh*, Mum,' I said, agonized, because we were still at the school gates and anyone could hear us.

Kim and Melanie and Sarah weren't that far behind. They all had their mouths pressed together. Their big new joke.

'Did Mrs Edwards give that Kim a good telling off?' said Mum.

'Mmm. Please, Mum. Don't let's talk about it now,' I hissed.

Mum looked back over her shoulder.

'That's her, isn't it? The tall girl with the black fringe. Well, she doesn't look very sorry. She's got a smirk all over her face,' said Mum. 'Maybe I'd better have a few words with that young madam.'

'Mum, *no*! Please, please, please,' I begged. 'Mrs Edwards sorted it all out and they've promised they won't say anything else.'

'Are you *sure*, Mandy?' said Mum. 'You still look very bothered, darling.'

'I'm not bothered a bit,' I said, trying to smile and act bouncy.

And then I saw Tanya at the end of the road, pushing the baby. Tanya, in her shortest shorts and a tiny top showing off her navel, her high heels clacking at each step.

'Tanya!'

'Hey, Mandy!'

I went charging up the road to greet her. She did that high-five hand thing so I did it too.

'How was school then, eh?' she said.

I pulled a face.

'I get you,' said Tanya. 'It's great for me, eh? I don't have to go because it's nearly the summer holidays. Not that I ever go much. I can't stick school. All them stupid teachers. And silly cows calling you names.'

'They call *you* names?' I said, astonished.

'Yeah, but I call them worse stuff,' said Tanya, grinning. 'Why, anyone giving you hassle, Mandy?'

'Oooh,' I said vaguely.

Kim and Sarah and Melanie were already past Mum, who was puffing in the background. They were staring at Tanya and me. Melanie practically had her mouth hanging open.

Tanya saw me glance at them. She had it all sussed out in a second.

She ignored Sarah and Melanie. They were small fry, beneath her. She looked straight at Kim.

'What you staring at then?'

she said. She wasn't as tall as Kim even in her high heels, but she was older and much much tougher.

'Nothing,' Kim mumbled.

'Good. Well run off home, little girlies. Leave me and my pal Mandy in peace, eh?'

They cleared off. Even Kim. Their faces! Me and my pal Mandy. *I* was Tanya's friend. I was sure they were green with envy.

'I'm taking his Lordship for a walk round the park,' said Tanya. 'Coming?'

I was desperate to go, but when Mum reached us she wouldn't hear of us going there by ourselves.

'No, you can get funny men hanging around there,' said Mum. 'It's no place for young girls on their own.'

'I'll look after your Mandy, don't worry,' said Tanya.

'Thank you, dear, but I really don't think so. Mandy had better come home with me and have her tea,' said Mum.

'Oh, Mum, please, I've *got* to go to the park,' I begged.

'We can have ice creams if she's peckish,' said Tanya, jingling coins in her tiny pocket. 'Mrs Williams gave me some spending money. Oh, please, Mrs White, go on, say yes.'

'No, dear. Perhaps another day,' said Mum, taking hold of my hand.

I pulled it away.

'I want to *today*, Mum. It's not fair. Why do you have to treat me like a baby all the time?' I said.

Mum blinked at me, looking hurt. But she seemed to be wavering.

I was suddenly inspired.

'Mrs Edwards said I should try to be a bit more independent,' I said. 'She thinks I'm too young for my age and that's why the others pick on me.'

'Don't be silly, Mandy,' said Mum, but she sounded uncertain.

Maybe Mrs Edwards really had said something of the sort!

'We'll be back in half an hour,' said Tanya.

Mum sighed. 'All right, all right. If you really want to go to the park, Mandy, we'll walk along with Tanya.'

I took a deep breath.

'No. You don't have to come, Mum. There's not even any main roads or anything. And we'll keep away from any funny men. All the others go up the park by themselves. Not with their *mums*.'

I couldn't believe it was me saying it. Miranda Rainbow had taken over my mouth. And it worked! Mum *let* me go to the park with Tanya, though she didn't look at all happy about it. I knew she'd be hurt and huffy all evening but for once I didn't care.

Tanya and I ran across the grass, little Ricky jiggling up and down in his pram. Tanya sang old Nirvana songs and I tried to copy her. Ricky burbled a bit too, but then the bumping got a bit much for him.

'Yuck. Baby Ricky's been a bit sicky,' said Tanya.

She mopped him up with a tissue, wrinkling her nose, and then washed her hands in the paddling pool.

'My dad used to take me here when I was little,' I said. 'Sometimes he used to roll up his trouser legs and come in with me.'

'Your dad sounds nice,' said Tanya.

'Mmm. But my mum's a bit . . .' I pulled a face.

I was scared Tanya might tease me about Mum.

'She fusses because she cares about you,' said Tanya, surprisingly. '*I* used to fuss about Carmel heaps.'

'Do you miss her a lot?'

'Yeah,' said Tanya, folding her arms and hunching over. But then she straightened up again. 'Still, I've got you instead now, haven't I, young Mandy?'

'I'm not *young* Mandy,' I protested.

Tanya laughed and pulled my plait.

'You look about six with these.'

'Don't. It's not my fault. I begged my mum to let me have it up the way you did it, but she wouldn't do it.'

'You should learn to fix it yourself,' said Tanya.

We walked up and down slowly, rocking Ricky until he nodded off to sleep. Tanya parked him carefully in the shade.

'But we can do a spot of sunbathing, eh, Mandy?'

She kicked off her sandals and lay back on the grass, pulling up her top even more.

'I've got to get my tummy brown,' she said.

'I don't go brown, I just go pink,' I said, lying down beside her. 'I hate pink. It's my least favourite colour in all the world.'

'Well, we'll just lie in the sun for two

minutes. We don't want you burning,' said Tanya.

I didn't care if I frizzled into a crisp. I wanted to stay lying next to Tanya in the sun forever. I stared up at the green leaves far above us. They rustled, as if they were sharing a secret.

'Oh, Tanya, I'm so happy I've got you for my friend,' I said.

'Ah, you're sweet,' said Tanya. She sat up. 'Hey, you're going pink already. We'd better cool you down. Let's go and buy ice creams.'

We went to the kiosk at the park gates. Tanya bought us a small 99 cone each. Ricky wailed enviously, so Tanya put a little swirl of ice cream on her finger so he could lick it off. He liked this game and moaned for more.

'No, greedy guts. You'll make yourself sick again,' said Tanya. 'Come on, Mandy. We'd better get you home. Can't have your mum fussing.'

We walked along companionably, both of us pushing the pram. Tanya's heels went clack and my Clarks shoes squeaked. Her shadow was bouncy, with fancy hair. Mine was smaller and plodding and plaited.

'Hey, mind Ricky for me while I get Pat her paper,' said Tanya, when we got to the corner shop.

I stood outside, gently rocking Ricky, feeling great to be left in charge of a baby. I peered into the shop to watch Tanya. It was shadowy after the sunlight. I could just make her out, fiddling in her shorts pocket to get the right change for the *Evening Standard*. She handed it over, she took the paper, she walked towards the door.

Then her hand reached out, quick as a wink. She snatched something off a shelf and carried on sauntering straight out of the shop.

'Hey, Mandy. Got you a little present,' said Tanya, holding out her hand.

It was a green, velvet, crinkled hairband.

BLUE

Blue

Tanya brushed out my hair when we got back to my house and fixed the green velvet band into place.

'It's called a scrunchie,' said Tanya. 'There! Looks great, eh?'

'Yeah. Great. Thank you ever so much, Tanya,' I said. 'I love my scrunchie.'

My tummy felt as if it was all scrunched up, too. It was so lovely of Tanya to give it to me. She was the best friend in all the world. But she'd *stolen* it.

Well, I didn't know that for certain. It *looked* as if she'd snatched it straight off the shelf. But I hadn't been able to see properly. She might have paid for it with the money in her pocket.

I could ask her straight out. But I didn't dare. It would sound so awful.

'Thanks for my present, Tanya. By the way, did you pay for it or did you steal it?'

And if she *had* stolen it, then what?

I knew it was wrong to steal things. Especially from people like Mr and Mrs Patel, who didn't make very much money out of their corner shop. Although it was only a hairband. A little, velvet, scrunchie hairband that only cost a pound or two. It wasn't as if it was really valuable.

Tanya hadn't stolen it for herself. She'd stolen it for me, because I was her friend. And she didn't have any spare cash of her own. She didn't get proper pocket money every Saturday like me. She had hardly anything at all. So it wasn't really too awful for her to take it, was it?

I felt dizzy with all these conflicting thoughts buzzing round in my head. The scrunchie held my hair up tightly, pulling the little hairs at the nape of my neck. Every time I turned my head it gave me a painful little tweak, so that I couldn't forget about it.

It was almost a relief when Mum made me brush my hair back into its old style after Tanya had gone over the road.

'I know you think you look wonderful, Mandy,' said Mum, snorting. 'But I don't think that style really suits you.'

'I think she looks very grown-up,' said Dad, seeing me drooping.

Mum frowned. 'That's just the point. Mandy's still a little girl. That style's much too sophisticated. And a bit common, if you must know.'

'Still, it was very kind of Tanya to give Mandy that hair thingy,' said Dad.

'Mmm,' said Mum. 'Did she buy it for you specially, Mandy?'

'Yes,' I mumbled. I pretended to yawn. 'I'm ever so sleepy. I think I'll go to bed.'

I just wanted to get away from Mum and Dad. But I couldn't get to sleep. I lay awake fingering the scrunchie. I didn't know if you could buy them everywhere, or just in the corner shop. What if it was a special one – and Mrs Patel realized one was missing from her shelf? What if she'd even seen Tanya take it? What if she saw me wearing the green velvet scrunchie? Did that make me a thief, because I knew it was stolen?

When I eventually got to sleep I dreamt about it. Mrs Patel stopped me in the street and called me a thief. Mr Patel came out of the shop and he called me a thief too. Everyone in the street started staring. There were people from school there. Mrs Stanley and Mrs Edwards shaking their heads and looking very stern. Kim and Melanie and Sarah were standing in a row, chanting 'Thief, thief, thief', their teeth gleaming. And Mum and Dad were there, and they were saying it too, and they were crying, and I was crying too . . .

I woke up in a sweat, still hearing the word thief ringing in my ears. It was the middle of the night now, and the dark made it even more scary. I got up and shoved the scrunchie right at the back of my underwear drawer. Then I lay down again and tried hard to play a pretend game. I was Miranda Rainbow and she never lay awake in a blue funk at nights; she slept soundly in her rainbow sheets, a different colour for every day, and then she got up and had a soak in her jacuzzi and then she got dressed in . . . I tried on various imaginary outfits as if I was a paper doll, and eventually fell asleep again.

I stayed being Miranda Rainbow in my dream and I was still trying on different clothes because I was a famous fashion model now, and I strode up and down the catwalk while the

cameras flashed and everything ~~was won~~
derful but then I had to put on this new ~~o~~
a green, velvet, tight dress with a big matching
hairband, a huge scrunchie almost like a pull-
on hat, and everyone saw me wearing it and
suddenly stood up and started yelling 'Thief!'

and I tried to take the
scrunchie off but it
was too tight, it was
tied so tightly round
my head I could
hardly breathe, it
was right over my
eyes and blocking my
nose and gagging my
mouth so that I couldn't even scream . . .

I woke up gasping and sobbing, stuck right
down under the bedclothes. I must have made
a noise after all because Mum came running.

'Whatever's the matter, darling?'

'I – I just had a horrid dream,' I said, wiping
my face with the sheet.

'Hey, don't do that! Let's find you a hankie,
you poor little moppet,' said Mum, cuddling me
close. 'What was this horrid dream about, eh?'

'I can't remember,' I lied, clinging to Mum.
'But it was just so scary.'

'There. Mummy's here now,' said Mum,
rocking me.

She tucked me up tight with Olivia Orang-

Utan and promised me I'd go straight back to sleep and I wouldn't have any more bad dreams.

I tried to believe her. But it didn't work out that way. I was still awake when Dad's alarm went off in the morning.

I felt horrible and headachy at breakfast.

'You and your nightmares,' said Mum. 'Poor old Mandy.' She pulled my plaits fondly.

'Where's the trendy new hairstyle?' said Dad.

Mum frowned at him. 'I think Mandy's seen sense. It's not really suitable.' Mum folded her arms. 'I'm not too sure about this friendship with Tanya, you know. Mandy's started seeing such a lot of her. She's much too old for Mandy. She's a bad influence.'

'What do you mean?' I asked hoarsely.

'Well, you're starting to act really cheeky at times, Mandy. All that business after school yesterday ... I hate the idea of you going to that park with Tanya. Nowhere's safe nowadays.'

'I think young Tanya can look after herself – *and* our Mandy,' said Dad.

'I'm still not at all keen on them being so friendly. I don't mind Mandy having Tanya over here where I can keep an eye on things, but I don't want them going off together and getting into mischief,' said Mum. 'It's a bit of a risk, a girl with Tanya's background. I've a good mind to stop Mandy seeing her altogether.'

I stiffened. 'No!'

'Oh, come on,' said Dad. 'The girls are good friends. It's great to see Mandy having a bit of fun. And she needs a friend right now, especially after all this bullying business at school.'

That sidetracked Mum.

'Has all that stopped now, Mandy?' she asked. 'Kim doesn't say nasty things to you now?'

'She doesn't say anything now,' I said.

'Well, you keep well out of their way,' said Mum.

I did my best. They didn't hang round near me and whisper things that morning. It looked as if Tanya had scared them off.

She'd been so great to stand up to them like that. She was a truly wonderful friend. And she'd only taken that green hairband as a special present for me. I'd been silly to get so worked up about it. Why did I have to be such a goody-goody baby all the time?

I sat next to Arthur King at lunchtime and then afterwards he tried to teach me how to play chess. It got ever so boring. I wanted to let my mind wander and think about Tanya meeting me from school and how we were going to be friends for ever and ever.

'No, *look*, if you put your queen there I'll be able to take it with my knight,' said Arthur.

I couldn't get worked up about it. The queen

didn't have long hair and a flowing dress, the knight didn't have shining armour and a plume in his helmet. They were just twirly pieces of plastic with no personality whatsoever.

Arthur beat me so easily at chess that it wasn't even fun for him.

'Don't you like chess, Mandy?' he said, setting up the pieces again.

'Not really, no,' I said.

'Maybe you'll like it when you get better at it,' said Arthur. 'I was kind of hoping we could play every lunchtime.'

'Mmm,' I said vaguely.

'And if you're with me then Kim and Melanie and Sarah will keep away,' said Arthur.

'You what?'

'I think I've scared them off,' said Arthur. 'They won't do anything if I'm here to look after you.'

'Oh, Arthur!' I said, too amazed to be tactful. He was the cleverest boy in our class but he was also the dimmest too. 'That's nothing to do with you. It's because of my friend Tanya.'

Arthur looked wounded. 'How can it be this Tanya friend of yours? She's not here. Though it sometimes feels as though she is.'

'What do you mean?'

'Well, you just keep yap yap yapping about her. My friend Tanya says this. My friend Tanya says that. On and on. And it isn't even

90

as if she ever says anything that sounds remotely interesting. It's all make-up and clothes and what-the-stars-say and that rubbish.'

'Are you saying my friend Tanya talks rubbish?' I said indignantly.

'I don't know. I've never talked to her myself. But you just talk rubbish now, when you yack on about her.'

'Well, you can play your silly chess games by yourself, then,' I said, and I slammed down the pocket set with such force that all the remaining pieces jumped out of their holes and bounced on the black and white squares.

I stalked off by myself, though I knew it was a mistake. I wandered the playground for a bit and then I went to the girls' toilets. That was the biggest mistake of all. Kim and Sarah and Melanie were standing in front of the mirror, combing their hair, experimenting with new styles. Kim was brushing her black fringe back, exposing her startlingly white forehead. She caught my eye in the mirror and stopped brushing, her hand frozen in mid-air. Her fringe slowly flicked forward strand by strand until it was back in place.

I should have run for it. But I tried to make out I wasn't afraid. I marched straight past and went into one of the toilets and slammed the door. Then I sat on the loo, my heart thumping crazily.

'There's that girl we don't talk to,' said Kim. 'We don't even say her name, do we?'

'That's right. It's a stupid name anyway,' said Sarah.

'Well, she's a stupid girl,' said Melanie, giggling. 'And she's a sneaky tell-tale. She went blab-blab-blabbing to her mum and then she gets on to my mum and I get into trouble. My mum keeps trying to make me be friends with her again.'

'Yuck, friends with her,' said Sarah.

'That girl's got a new friend now, though,' said Kim silkily. 'A friend who thinks she's It. Well, she's It, all right. If It equals Filthy Slag.'

That unstoppered my mouth.

'Don't you dare call my friend Tanya a slag!' I shouted from inside the toilet.

They all burst out laughing.

'Did you see the colour of the Filthy Slag's hair? Bright orange. Like she's got a heap of dead goldfish sticking out of her head,' said Kim.

They laughed harder.

'And those high heels she had on! Wibble-wobble, wibble-wobble.'

I heard the three of them stomping about, in crude imitation.

'It's a wonder That Girl's Mumsie lets her go around with the Filthy Slag,' said Melanie.

'Well, they're all mumsies together, aren't they? The Filthy Slag had her little baby slagling in its pram,' said Kim.

'You're talking rubbish!' I shouted, unlocking the toilet door and charging out to confront them. 'That baby isn't *Tanya's*. She just helps look after it. And she's not a slag. She doesn't even go with boys. She can't stick them. So shut up, all of you.' I tried to sound fierce, but my voice was too high, and my eyes were full of tears. Several spilled over and dribbled down my cheeks. They all saw.

'Can you hear a little gnat squeaking?' said Kim.

'What, that little flea that's just come out the toilet?' said Sarah.

'She's a dirty little flea – she didn't even pull the chain,' said Melanie.

I hadn't even used the toilet but they all pulled faces, and Kim held her nose.

I did run then. Crying. And they laughed a lot more.

I kept wanting to cry all afternoon at school. I peered desperately across the room at Arthur, but he wouldn't look at me. I scribbled a little note:

Dear Arthur
I'm sorry. I was a silly pig.
Mandy
P.S. I hope none of your chess pieces are missing.

I folded it up and printed *Arthur King* on the front. I tried to lean past Melanie to get the girl the other side of her to pass it to Arthur. Melanie was too quick. She snatched the note and opened it up and read it. Then she passed it to Kim and Sarah. They were all grinning like anything. Kim wrinkled up her nose and made little snorty pig noises, pointing at me. Melanie and Sarah copied her.

I bent my head over my English exercises. I pressed on my pen so hard I broke the nib and I had to carry on with a blotchy ballpoint. A big tear splashed on the page, making the ink blur. There was another tear, and another, until my page was like a puddle. I felt I was drowning in my own deep blue sea. Kim and Melanie and Sarah snorted and sniggered back in the shallows.

'Who's making that stupid snorting noise?' said Mrs Stanley impatiently.

She looked round at us. I hunched up, scared she'd see my watery eyes. My nose was watery too, and I had to blow it.

'It's only Mandy, Mrs Stanley, blowing her nose,' said Kim.

Melanie and Sarah laughed. Some of the others joined in too.

'Don't be so silly,' said Mrs Stanley, sighing. 'I think I'd better sober you all up. Get out your rough books. We'll have a little spelling test.'

There was a terrible groan. Most of the class looked at me as if it was somehow my fault.

Mrs Stanley called out the words. They looked wrong no matter which way round I put the letters. We had to swap our papers with our next-door neighbour for marking. Melanie. We had to stay work-partners even though she'd stopped being my friend and become my second-worst enemy. Mrs Stanley wasn't the sort of teacher who would ever let you swap seats.

So I had to give my spelling paper to Melanie

and she had to take mine. She just held the very edge of my paper as if it was all dirty and germy, and she threw it quickly down on her desk. Kim and Sarah giggled appreciatively.

I only got twelve out of twenty. Melanie ringed all my mistakes with red pen and made giant crosses. It was my worst ever test. Melanie got fourteen. Kim got eighteen. She came top. She even beat Arthur.

We had to read out our marks to Mrs Stanley. She looked very surprised when I mumbled mine. I thought she might get a bit cross, but she didn't say anything. Then she called me to her desk when the bell rang.

'Is anything the matter, Mandy?' she said.

I shook my head and stared at the floor.

'What happened with your spelling test, hmm? Melanie did mark it properly, didn't she?'

I nodded.

'Are Melanie and Kim and Sarah still saying silly things, Mandy?'

'No, Mrs Stanley,' I said. Well they weren't saying them to me. Just *about* me. But now they didn't say my name I couldn't prove it was me they were talking about. Kim was so clever.

Mrs Stanley didn't look as if she believed me one hundred per cent, but she sighed and said I could go.

Mum was waiting outside, starting to get anxious. But there was no sign of Tanya.

'There you are, Mandy! Why are you so late, darling? The others all came out a good five minutes ago. You didn't get kept in, did you?'

'No, it was just . . . Mrs Stanley was just saying . . . oh, it doesn't matter. Mum, where's Tanya?'

'*What* was Mrs Stanley saying? Never mind Tanya.'

'Just about *spelling*. Boring boring spelling. I thought Tanya was coming to meet me again? She said she was last night.'

'But you're excellent at spelling! You always learn your words perfectly. Look, I thought it would be nice if you and I went into the town and did a bit of shopping. I was in Maxwell's and they've got some lovely pink gingham frocks with smocking on the front—'

'Yuck!'

'Don't talk like that, Mandy! I hate that expression.'

'But I can't go shopping, Mum, I promised I'd see Tanya.'

'Yes, and I told Tanya that you and I were going shopping.'

'Ooooh! But I'd much much much sooner see Tanya,' I said.

Mum's head jerked, as if I'd slapped her face.

My tummy went all squelchy. It wasn't fair. Any girl would sooner have fun with her friend than trail round the shops with her mum.

'Oh well, if you really don't want to, then I suppose I can't force you,' Mum said shakily. 'But you do need some new summer frocks and we haven't had a little jaunt after school for a long time. I thought we'd maybe treat you to an ice cream at the Soda Fountain . . .'

'Couldn't you have asked Tanya to come along too?' I said.

Mum took a deep breath, her nostrils pinched.

'I don't really think that would be a good idea, Mandy,' said Mum. 'You've been seeing more than enough of Tanya recently. Goodness gracious, she's hanging around every day now, the two of you shut up in that bedroom. Daddy and I hardly ever get to see you.'

'That's not true! And anyway—'

'Look, I don't want a silly argument, Mandy. Are we going to go shopping and have a lovely time – or not?'

We went shopping. But we didn't have a lovely time. I absolutely hated the pink dresses in Maxwell's. They were so little-girly it just wasn't true. The size that fitted me was for an eight-year-old anyway. I looked eight in it. No, *younger*.

'But you look lovely, darling,' said Mum,

down on her knees in the changing-room, tweaking the hem and tying the dinky bow at the back. 'We could get you pink and white ribbons to match to wear on your plaits.'

'Yuck!'

'Mandy! How many more times do I have to tell you?'

'Well, it *is* a yucky idea, Mum. I don't want to have my hair in plaits any more, they look stupid. Even Dad thinks so. And *I* look stupid in this silly baby frock.'

'I think you're the one acting like a silly baby,' said Mum. 'Well, all right. You don't have to have the pink frock. Which one did you like? What about the one with the cherries, with the embroidered collar? Shall we try that one on?'

'I don't want a frock at all. No-one wears them any more.'

'I see,' said Mum, meaning she didn't. 'So everyone goes out in just their vest and knickers, is that right?'

'No. Girls wear . . . shorts.'

Mum snorted. 'If you think I'm going to let you wander round wearing shorts like Tanya then you've got another think coming.'

'I don't mean just Tanya,' I said, though I did. 'All the girls in my class wear shorts and jeans and leggings.'

'Yes, well, I don't think you suit that sort of style,' said Mum.

'I *want* to suit it, though. I want to look like the others. That's why they keep picking on me. Because I'm different,' I wailed.

 That made Mum waver a bit. So I kept it up. And in the end she bought me a pair of shorts and a T-shirt. Long shorts. *Pink*. But at least they *were* shorts. She bought me a new swimming costume too. Dad and I go swimming every Sunday morning. I begged for a bikini. I thought that way I could wear the bikini top with my shorts. I knew that would look great. But Mum laughed at me.

'A bikini! Honestly, Mandy, you're as straight up and down as an ironing board!'

She bought me a boring little-girl costume. She couldn't pick pink again because they didn't come in that colour. I wanted bright orange but Mum said it was too loud. She chose a blue costume with a silly little white bow at the front and two buttons in the shape of white rabbit heads.

'You look so sweet,' said Mum, trying hard to pretend we were having a lovely time after all.

Mum wasn't even cross when I showed her my broken pen. We went down to Maxwell's stationery department and mum bought me a new ink pen and a matching propelling pencil.

I was desperate to go home right away after the shopping spree but Mum wanted me to have a treat at the Soda Fountain. So we went there and I chose a Cherry Special and I sucked cherries and licked cream and churned the ice cream round and round in the silver dish because somehow it didn't taste right.

Tanya was waiting for me when we got back home at long last. She was perched on the little picket fence round our garden.

Mum sighed as I sped ahead.

'I don't think that fence is really strong enough to sit on, Tanya,' Mum called.

'Yeah, it's not very comfy,' said Tanya, getting up and rubbing the red ridges on her thighs. 'Hey, what're all these carrier bags? Have you been getting presents, Mandy? You lucky thing!'

Oh, how I wished we'd bought Tanya a present! Especially when she'd given me the green hairband.

'Here, we've got you a little present, Tanya,' I said quickly, and I snatched the propelling pencil out of its bag and gave it to her.

Mum raised her eyebrows but she didn't say anything.

'Oh, wow! A present for me! A pencil, oh *great*, I've never had one of these posh pro-pelling ones before. Thanks *ever* so,' said Tanya, and she kissed me. She even reached up and kissed Mum.

'Right – so what have you got, eh?' Tanya said, delving in the bags.

'Oh, they're *lovely*!' she said, holding up my new T-shirt and shorts.

Mum looked surprised but pleased.

'What do you mean, "lovely"?' I muttered to Tanya. 'You wouldn't wear them.'

'Yes, but they'll look great on you,' said Tanya.

'Thanks!' I said, giving her a little push.

'And what else have you got?' said Tanya, rooting in the other bags. 'Oh, a pen like my pencil! And what's this?'

'Just a swimming costume.'

'Let's see. Oh, I like the little bunnies.'

I squinted at her through my glasses, still not sure whether she was acting or not.

'Can you swim then, Mandy?'

'Oh yes, Mandy goes swimming with her father every Sunday,' said Mum, fussing with the clothes, folding them back into their bags. 'Come on, Mandy, indoors. We must get tea.'

'Did your dad teach you to swim, Mandy? Will he teach me? Can I come on Sunday too?'

'Oh, yes!' I said joyfully.

'We'll see,' said Mum.

I knew what 'we'll see' meant. It was a polite way of saying no.

But Dad seemed keen on the idea. 'Yes, of course young Tanya can come along too,' he said.

I whooped triumphantly.

'I'm not sure that's such a good plan,' Mum called from the kitchen. 'That Tanya is starting to tag around after Mandy everywhere.'

'She doesn't tag. I'm the one who tags round after her,' I insisted.

'Now calm down, Mandy,' said Mum, coming into the hall in her apron. 'Goodness, let Daddy change his work clothes and get comfy first before you start pestering him. We'll discuss this swimming later on.'

'There's nothing to discuss, Mum. Dad said *yes*,' I said.

He went on saying yes even though Mum tried hard to make him change his mind.

'I know you seem to have taken such a shine to Tanya – but I'm really worried about her. I've been talking to Mrs Williams and Tanya comes from a really *dreadful* background.'

Mum started whispering to Dad. I tried to hear. I kept waiting for the word thief.

Dad saw me biting my lip.

'Yes, OK, poor old Tanya. It sounds as if she's had a really tough time,' said Dad. 'So shouldn't we try to be extra kind to her, then? Show her what life in a normal loving family is like? She seems a surprisingly nice girl, considering – and very fond of our Mandy. So where's the harm in their friendship? You keep saying Tanya might be a bad influence on Mandy. Have you ever thought that Mandy might be a *good* influence on Tanya?'

I punched the air in triumph. Dad had beaten Mum well and truly.

So we went swimming on Sunday, Dad and Tanya and me. Tanya didn't seem quite so keen on the idea at first. We called for her at half past seven and Mrs Williams said she was still in bed, though she'd called her twice.

Tanya appeared ten minutes later, white-faced and yawning, her orange hair sticking up on end. It was the first time I'd ever seen her without make-up. She looked astonishingly different. Much younger. Softer. More easily hurt.

Dad had been getting irritable hanging about waiting for her, but now he smiled.

'Morning, Tanya!'

'Morning! It feels like it's still the middle of the night,' she said. But she smiled back at Dad. And then she stuck out her tongue at me. 'What are you staring at, eh?' She rubbed her strangely-bare eyes and combed her hair with her fingers. 'I look a sight, don't I?'

'I think you look lovely,' I said.

I thought Tanya would probably have a bikini but when we changed at the baths she put on an old faded navy costume, plain and ordinary.

'I haven't got my own costume. This was Mrs Williams' daughter's school thingy. Isn't it foul? Look, there are all these little holes.' Tanya poked at them with her finger. 'I'm going to get arrested for indecency!'

'It looks fine,' I insisted. '*I'm* the one who looks an idiot.' I tweaked my bow and the stupid bunny heads.

'You look cute,' said Tanya. She sounded wistful. 'You're lucky, your mum doesn't half spoil you. Doesn't she come swimming too?'

I looked at Tanya. We both had a mental image of my mum in a tight bathing costume. We grinned guiltily. 'Perhaps not,' said Tanya.

We stowed our clothes in the same locker. I liked it that my new T-shirt and shorts were curled up with Tanya's top and leggings. I had to leave my glasses behind too. It's always so strange taking them off. The whole world mists over and disappears in the distance. I have to half-feel my way to the swimming pool and all I can see is brilliant, sparkling blue.

'Here, I'll help you,' said Tanya, and she held

my hand tight. 'Where's your dad? Oh, there he is, standing on the edge. Hey, are you going to dive?' She hurried us over to him, our bare feet pattering on the damp tiles. 'Bet you can't dive!' she said.

'Bet I can,' said Dad, just like a schoolboy. And then he dived in and swam away, his arms smoothly dipping through the water, his pointed feet kicking, until I lost him in the turquoise blur.

'Hey, he can! What an old show-off, eh?' said Tanya, laughing at him.

Dad was laughing too when he swam back. He pulled himself up onto the side and sat kicking his legs, little beads of water shining all over him. I was worried about his soft fat tummy and all the hairs on his chest. Grey hairs. But Tanya seemed to think he was some sort of Super-Dad.

'Hey, show *me* how to dive. You're great at it! And I want to swim all smooth like that too, I just splash.' She kept on, but she took ages and ages actually getting into the water herself. Dad had to hold her hands and coax her down the steps. I jumped in. Then even after Tanya was in the water she wouldn't duck down and get her shoulders wet. She stood shivering with her arms wrapped round herself, and when Dad tried to show her how to swim the crawl Tanya wasn't sure she could do it, and remembered she'd had an ear infection and maybe she shouldn't get her head wet.

Dad didn't try and make her do anything. We played bouncing in the water instead, just Dad and me at first, but then we caught hold of Tanya's hands and she bounced too. She shrieked ever so loudly to begin with, but then she started liking it and laughing.

'We're the bouncy family,' she said, as we did a mad ring-a-ring-a-roses. She sang, 'We are the boun-cy fam-i-ly. There's Mandy's dad and Mandy and me.'

We all sang Tanya's song over and over, whirling round in the blue water. 'I wish we really were a proper family,' I said. 'I'd give anything to have you as my sister, Tanya.'

'Yeah, you're like my little sister now,' said Tanya. 'And we'll always stay together and no-one shall ever split us up, right?'

INDIGO

Indigo

School was still horrible. Kim and Melanie and Sarah started holding their noses whenever I went past. Some of the others copied them. Not Arthur. But he was still a bit huffy. I tried not to care. I stalked past with my head in the air, being Miranda Rainbow until Kim stuck her foot out and I tripped.

She didn't try anything when there were any teachers around. Mrs Edwards was stepping up her Anti-Bullying Campaign. 'Wait till the holidays,' Kim said loudly to Melanie. 'Then we'll get her. Round at your place.'

My mum still had this arrangement with Melanie's mum. I went round there every morning in the holidays while Mum worked.

'But I *can't* go to Melanie's now,' I insisted.

'Have they started bullying you again?' said Mum.

'No. Well, not really. They just do silly things sometimes. But don't go back to the school, Mum! I just ignore them like you told me. But I absolutely can't go to Melanie's in the holidays. She hates me. And I hate her, too.'

Mum got very worried. She wanted me to try to make friends with Melanie again.

'But Mandy doesn't *want* to be friends with Melanie,' said Dad. 'And I don't blame her. Melanie's been horrible to her.'

'They used to get on all right. I just don't know what to do otherwise,' said Mum wretchedly. 'I can't take Mandy to the office with me. She's not old enough to be left on her own. But she's *too* old for a child-minder. What on earth are we going to do?'

'It's obvious!' said Dad.

'You mean I should give in my notice?' said Mum.

'No! Have a word with Mrs Williams. I'm sure she'd be happy to keep on eye on Mandy. Then she and Tanya could keep each other company.'

'Oh, yes! *Yes*! YES!' I shouted.

Mum said no. She went on and on saying no.

She tried to find someone else to look after me. But in the end she gave up and fixed it with Mrs Williams after all.

'Oh, Mum, how wonderful!' I said, capering about the room.

'Hey, hey, calm down, you'll knock something over! Now listen to me, Mandy. I want you to behave yourself when you're at Mrs Williams. I'm not having you running wild with Tanya. There are going to be lots of rules, all right?'

'To hear is to obey, O Great Mother,' I said.

We didn't obey any of Mum's rules. Mrs Williams didn't seem to mind much what we did as long as we didn't play music too loudly when the babies were having their naps. She let us go off round the town together and she didn't even get mad if we were late back.

'You are lucky, Tanya,' I said without thinking as we walked into town arm in arm. 'Mrs Williams doesn't ever nag at you and make you stick to rules and tell you off like my mum.'

'Well. That's because she's not my mum,' said Tanya. 'She's just my foster mum. She gets paid for looking after me. It's her job. And she didn't even want me, I was just shoved her way because they couldn't find anywhere else for me. We get on OK, she's not a bad old stick, but she doesn't really care about me. She gets all gooey-eyed over the babies sometimes. I don't know *why* because they're all slurpy and snotty most of the time. But she couldn't care less about me. So she doesn't nag. Your mum nags because she's absolutely dotty about you, anyone can see that. She loves you to bits.'

I didn't know what to say.

'And your dad thinks the world of you too,' said Tanya, more enviously.

'What about your dad, Tanya?' I said.

She'd never really mentioned him.

'Him!' said Tanya, snorting. 'Haven't seen him for donkey's years. Don't want to.'

She unlinked arms and walked on quickly, her sandals clacking. I had to hurry to keep up. She had her face turned away from me. She looked as if she was trying not to cry.

'I'm sorry, Tanya,' I said worriedly.

'What are you sorry for?' she said, sounding fierce.

'Well. I didn't mean to upset you. About your dad.'

'I'm not upset. I don't give a toss about him. Or my mum, not any more. Or even my little brothers, because they've been adopted now and they're doing great. It's just Carmel . . .'

'Won't they let you see her?' I asked.

'We had this supervised visit at Easter but she got all shy and her foster mum was there and . . .' Tanya sniffed. 'Look, shut up, Mandy. I don't want to talk about it, OK?'

'OK,' I said.

'Don't look so down, dopey. Come on, let's get into the town and cheer ourselves up,' said Tanya.

We went into Boots, spending ages at the make-up counters. It was great fun at first. Tanya put all this sample eye shadow and lipstick on me and we squirted ourselves with tester perfume. But then Tanya started sauntering round the shelves – and I saw her hands reach out and grab. She was wearing a hooded sweatshirt with big pockets. It was easy for her to hide stuff.

I followed her, trembling all over. She wandered around, so cool, so casual. An expert.

We walked out the shop and I waited for the hand on her shoulders, the stern voice. But it didn't happen. We walked on, Tanya's eyes sparkling, a grin on her face. She'd cheered up all right.

'Hey Mandy, come on. Better get you to a Ladies. You look a right clown with all that make-up on your face,' said Tanya. She looked at me closely. 'What's up, eh?'

My throat was so dry I couldn't speak. I just stood there, shaking.

'Hey, want to see what I've got for you?' Tanya whispered.

She held open her pocket and showed me a can of hair spray.

'Told you that's what you need to fix your hair. When you put it up. Why don't you ever wear that scrunchie I got you, eh?'

I just shrugged and shook my head. I was so scared of upsetting her again, I didn't dare say anything about her shoplifting.

She started to do it every time we went shopping together. I still didn't dare say anything outright, but I tried my hardest to get her to stay in at Mrs Williams'.

'Please, Tanya. Shopping's boring. Let's stay in and we'll play your tapes or draw or something. Whatever you want. Please,' I begged.

Sometimes it worked. They were the most wonderful mornings ever. We played Tanya's tapes until even I was word perfect. I just mouthed the words though. Tanya sang in her dead-cool husky way, and she did all the right gestures and invented her own special little dances.

'Do you think I'll ever make it as a rock star, Mandy?' Tanya asked, wiggling away.

'You bet you will,' I said.

She dressed up like a rock star too in shiny shorts and a fantastic violet sparkly top that looked wonderful. She painted her lids with purple eyeshadow, doing lovely whirly patterns right up to her eyebrows. One time she took my box of felt-tip pens and designed amazing tattoos for her arms and legs – weird flowers with faces, prancing unicorns, and witches casting spells. She inked a dark purply-blue bracelet round her thin wrist and got me to help her draw a ring on every finger, studded with red rubies, green emeralds, purple amethysts and blue sapphires.

'Do me a tattoo, Tanya,' I pleaded.

'Your mum will create,' said Tanya, but she drew a tiny tattoo inside my wrist. The felt-tip tickled and it felt funny when she pressed on my veins. She drew a red heart outlined with a

frill. There were two names entwined, Tanya and Mandy. I felt faint with pride and happiness.

116

When it was time for Mum to come and collect me I stuck a plaster over my tattoo and pretended I'd scratched myself. Whenever I was on my own I'd take little peeks at the heart. I managed to keep it until bedtime and then Mum made me have a bath. The plaster peeled off and the heart got washed away.

I took my felt-tips with me the next day and demanded another heart. Tanya liked to draw too, using her new propelling pencil. We made up this really great story about two girls who travelled all round the world together. Tanya called her girl Love Tanyanita. I let mine be called Miranda Rainbow.

I was a little worried at first sharing such an important pretend person with Tanya but she took it all seriously and didn't tease at all.

Love and Miranda were poor at first and they had to hitch lifts in lorries and share a sleeping bag at the side of the road, but then Love started singing and had a hit album and made even more money than Madonna. She still stayed best friends with Miranda. They lived in a penthouse flat with white furniture and white carpets and a heart-shaped white bed and a huge swimming pool on the roof with real dolphins and when Love and Miranda travelled the world they now had their own white stretch limousine . . .

Tanya was so good at adding bits to the story that I begged her to write it all down for me so I could remember it all for ever.

'Ther wer to girls,' Tanya wrote, very slowly.

I didn't say a word. But she saw my expression.

'Yeah, well, I'm not that great at writing,' she said. 'I've had learning problems. Because of my mum and stuff. And I'm dyslexic anyway. Know what that is? It's when you can't read and write well. But it doesn't mean you're thick.'

'Of course not,' I said quickly.

'I can't be thick, because I know all the

words, great long ones, some of them. I just don't know how to write them down proper.'

'I could teach you!' I offered.

But it didn't work. I felt too shy to point out all Tanya's mistakes. When I dared tell her something was wrong she went red.

'Hey, this is boring! It's the holidays. Who wants to do school stuff in the holidays? Come on, let's go into the town.'

'No!'

'Oh, come on, Mandy, I'm fed up with staying in.'

'There's not time before my mum comes to collect me.'

'Don't be daft. Your mum doesn't come till half-one. Why don't you want to go shopping, eh?'

'You know why,' I said desperately.

'What?'

'Because . . . because I don't like it when you . . .'

'When I what?'

'You know.'

'No. So *tell* me,' said Tanya, doing up her sandals.

'When you . . . take things.'

Tanya stood up in her heels, her hands on her hips.

'But I always nick something nice for you too,' she said.

'Yes, but . . . I wish you wouldn't. I get so scared.

'Look, it's OK. I know what I'm doing. I won't get caught, honest. I never do.'

'But . . . it's wrong,' I said, nearly in tears.

'*What?*' said Tanya. 'Oh, give me a break.'

'It's stealing.'

'I know it's stealing. But they won't miss it. They mark the prices up to counteract any shoplifters. And how else am I going to get all the stuff I need, eh? Old Pat isn't exactly generous with the pocket money even though she gets paid a fortune for looking after me. It's OK for you to be Miss Goody-Goody. You get heaps of things bought for you.'

'I know. I'm sorry. Don't get mad at me, Tanya. OK. We'll go shopping,' I said tearfully.

'Oh, I've gone off the whole idea now,' said Tanya. 'You've just spoilt it all. I used to get things for Carmel and she was thrilled, she thought I was really great. We used to have such fun together. But you're no fun at all, Mandy White.'

She threw herself down on her bed and hid her face.

'Oh, Tanya, don't, please,' I said, sobbing now.

I couldn't believe everything had gone so terrifyingly wrong in just a few seconds. I could have bitten out my tongue.

Then Mrs Williams knocked at the door and poked her head round.

'Yes, I thought I heard someone crying! What's up, Mandy?'

'Nothing,' I said stupidly, although I was howling.

Mrs Williams looked at the bed.

'Is Tanya throwing a moody?' she said. 'Hey, Tanya?'

Tanya didn't move.

'Never mind,' said Mrs Williams. 'You come downstairs with me, Mandy. We'll have a cup of tea and a biscuit, OK?'

'But what about Tanya?'

'She'll come and join us when she feels like it,' said Mrs Williams.

I was sure she was wrong. I cried so much I couldn't gulp down my tea. Simon came and sat on my foot, staring up at me curiously. Charlie crawled over too, whining irritably himself because he was teething. Great drools ran down his chin. Baby Ricky started whimpering in his pram in the hall.

'Good heavens, you're a moany lot today,' said Mrs Williams. 'So what was the row about with you and Tanya, eh, Mandy?'

'Nothing,' I repeated, blowing my nose.

'Yeah, nothing,' said a familiar voice.

Tanya came clacking into the kitchen.

'I want a cup of tea too, Pat. And let's have

some chocky biscuits too, yeah?' She bent down and tickled Simon's tummy. 'We want chocky bickies, don't we, little pal?'

He giggled and squealed. Charlie clamoured for attention too and she swung him high above her head. He drooled with delight.

'Yuck, you're drenching me, you little waterspout,' said Tanya, putting him down again and wiping her face.

She looked at me.

'Hey, you're spouting too! What's up, Mandy?'

'Oh, Tanya,' I sobbed. 'Will you make friends?'

'We're always friends, you daft banana,' said Tanya, and she dabbed at my face with the dishcloth. 'Here, wipe your eyes.'

'We'll go shopping now,' I said.

'No, it's OK,' said Tanya, nibbling her chocolate biscuit. 'Maybe tomorrow.'

I decided I didn't care what Tanya did. I had to have her as my friend no matter what. Even if it meant she went shoplifting while we were out.

I got terribly scared all the same when the two of us set off for the town the next morning. Tanya looked at me closely.

'Are you all right?'

'Yes!' I said quickly, forcing a smile.

'Come on, tell old Tanya what's bugging you,' she said, tickling me under the chin as if I was Charlie.

'Give over,' I said, laughing too loudly.

I wanted so badly to show her I could be fun. Tanya might not be that great at reading words but she could read my mood just like that.

'It's OK, Mandy,' she said. 'Look, if it seriously bothers you I promise I won't nick any more stuff for you, OK?'

'Really?' I said, dizzy with relief.

'I'm not saying I won't nick any stuff for *me*, mind you,' said Tanya, grinning. She put her arm round me. 'You still want to be friends with me, yeah?'

'You're the best friend in the whole world,' I said fervently.

We went to the Flowerfields Shopping Centre and at first we had the greatest time ever. We larked around watching the animated mice and bunnies and squirrels dancing through the plastic flower display. Tanya fished out a whole handful of change from the wishing fountain – but then she threw it all back.

'Come on, make lots of wishes, Mandy,' she

said, scattering coins so fast the water plinked.

I wished that Tanya would be my friend forever.

I wished that Kim and Melanie and Sarah would stop teasing me when I went back to school.

I wished that I could turn into Miranda Rainbow.

I wished that wishes always came true.

'What did you wish for, Tanya?' I asked.

Tanya wiggled her nose. 'If I tell then it won't come true,' she said.

We wandered all round Flowerfields. We spent ages in the HMV shop listening to music.

Tanya fingered a new Kurt T-shirt wistfully. I held my breath. But she just gave it a little stroke.

'It's lovely, isn't it?' she said. 'I'll see if Pat will buy it for me. I need new clothes for the summer.'

'I've got some savings, Tanya. I could buy it for you as a present,' I said. I fumbled with my purse. 'I haven't got all my money with me today, Mum won't let me take it all out at once, but I've got nearly twenty pounds at home, honest.'

'You keep it, Mandy,' said Tanya, but she looked touched.

We went up in the glass bubble lift to the top floor. Tanya held my hand as we flew up in the lift together. I was so happy I felt as if we were flying right out in the air, soaring sky high. Then we stepped out into the top arcade and Tanya peered round, sussing out all the best shops.

'Hey, this looks good,' she said, tugging me along with her.

It was a shop called *Indigo*. I'd never been there but I'd heard Melanie going on and on about it. It had a dark blue front with silver slatted doors, the sort you get in a cowboy saloon. It was dark blue inside, with swirly silver lights. We looked strangely blue ourselves and we got the giggles.

All the clothes were on silver racks with special spotlights. They were mostly denim, jeans and shirts and little skirts and jackets, and there were some dark blue knitted sweaters too that Tanya went crazy over. She tried one on and whirled around, stroking its softness.

'I could buy you that instead,' I said.

Tanya wrinkled her eyebrows and showed me the price ticket.

'Wow! Well. I can't afford that,' I said.

'No-one can afford it,' said Tanya, looking at herself in the mirror.

There was a sales assistant across the shop, watching. A fair, good-looking boy dressed in *Indigo* clothes.

Tanya stuck her chest out.

'Honestly, look at that guy giving me the eye,' she said, smirking a little.

'Maybe you're not supposed to try on the jumpers,' I said.

'How can you tell what they look like if you don't try them on,' said Tanya, struggling out of the sweater reluctantly.

She took her time folding it up. I watched her, my heart starting to beat fast. But she put it back on the shelf beside the others.

We went over to look at the jewellery in a case against the wall. We bent over the huge chunky silver bracelets and the rings studded with turquoises. The case was locked so we couldn't try them on.

'Shall I call that guy over, get him to open it for us?' said Tanya.

'No!'

'He's still staring at me.'

She stared back, a silly expression on her face.

'I thought you hated boys,' I said sourly.

'I do,' said Tanya. 'But I can't help it if they fancy me, can I?'

She walked over to a display of cowboy boots, so we were much nearer the fair boy. He had his arms folded, and he kept tossing his head to flick his fair hair out of his eyes. He was certainly still staring at Tanya. He had blue eyes. Dark blue. Indigo, like the shop. He looked the sort of boy you see in television soaps. The sort most girls are crazy about. Maybe even Tanya.

'Tanya, come on. We ought to be getting back soon, because of my mum,' I said sharply.

'We've got bags of time yet,' said Tanya. 'Come on, I want to try some of these cowboy boots. Aren't they great?'

She bent and undid one clompy sandal. Her foot wasn't very clean. She stuffed it quickly into a white studded boot.

'Terrific, eh?' said Tanya, waggling her leg admiringly. She looked up. 'Oh, oh!' she said.

The fair boy was coming over. Tanya winked at me and then smiled as the boy approached.

But he didn't smile back.

'Can you get us the other boot, eh?' said Tanya, her hand on her hip.

'No, I can't. And you can take that one off too. You kids have been messing about in the shop long enough. It's time you were going,' he said.

I felt myself flushing, nearly dying of embar- rassment. Tanya was red too as she tried to take off the boot. She lost her balance and nearly fell over.

'Look, stop clowning about,' said the boy. 'You shouldn't try on boots with bare feet. It's not hygienic.'

He sniffed as Tanya's grubby foot came out of the boot. Tanya said nothing at all. She didn't look at him. She didn't look at me. Her hands were shaking as she strapped her sandal. She turned and started walking out. I scrambled after her.

I saw her hand reach out to a shelf. I saw a blur of dark blue. And then it was gone, but Tanya's sweatshirt was suddenly straining over her stomach.

I tried to make my legs keep on walking. Out of the shop. Along the top arcade. Towards the lift.

But then someone shouted. Tanya turned.

The boy was coming after us.

'Run!' she yelled. *'Run!'*

VIOLET

Violet

We ran. We ran for our lives. There was no time to wait for the lift. We pounded along the upper arcade and then Tanya dived for the escalator. I threw myself after her, hurtling down the moving staircase, barging into cross women, zigzagging past those who wouldn't budge, bumping and jostling so that I banged hard against the rail and for one sickening moment felt I might topple over into thin air, down down down into the wishing well.

I screamed, and Tanya turned. She was already nearly at the bottom of the escalator. She could have carried on running. She'd have probably got clean away.

But she stopped. She started running *up* to me.

'I've got you,' she said, her fingers tight round my wrist.

My head cleared, the lights stopped whirling. I looked round. There were two security guards in blue uniform at the top of the escalator.

'Quick! I'm OK,' I gabbled, and I started running down again, we both did, pushing and shoving and dodging, down until we got to the bottom and they were still only halfway down after us.

'Run, then!' shouted Tanya.

We ran again, and my heart was banging in my chest and I had a stitch and my mouth tasted of metal but I kept on running. I ran as fast as Tanya, who was clopping like crazy in her sandals. The shopping centre was full and though it meant we had to keep pushing we were hidden from view half the time. We were getting near the entrance, skirting the plastic flowers, outrunning the rabbits and squirrels, getting nearer, getting there, getting away.

Tanya suddenly stopped dead. Her fingers

tightened on mine. I saw her staring. I saw what she was staring at. More security men, talking into their radios, spreading out. Waiting for us.

'Quick, into one of the shops,' said Tanya, darting.

But we weren't quite quick enough.

One of them spotted us, and moved fast. We turned and started running back into the centre but we were too late. There was a hand on my shoulder. Two hands, pinning my arms.

'Hang on now, little lady,' said a voice.

'Run, Tanya!' I screamed at her.

But they had her now too, one each side of her, and she was caught, I was caught, everyone was staring and pointing. I heard the word thief. I shook my head and I struggled and I kept trying to open my eyes up wide, because I so wanted it all to be another nightmare.

It couldn't really be happening.

'Come on now, stop struggling. We've got you. Don't make things worse for yourself. Let's go back to the shop on the top floor, eh?'

'Not her! Not the little one,' Tanya said. 'It's nothing to do with her. She's under age anyway. Let her go. Let her go, you pigs! You've got me, isn't that enough?'

But we were both taken back up in the glass bubble lift, and I couldn't believe that only fifteen minutes ago we'd been so happy and I'd felt we were flying. Now I had men holding me as if I was a criminal. And that's the way people were looking at me, looking at Tanya.

We were walked along the upper arcade and more people were looking and tutting and someone said it was a disgrace, kids running wild nowadays, and they blamed the mothers . . . and I thought about my mum and I started to cry.

'Now then, no need for tears. Don't be frightened, we're not going to hurt you,' said the security man, looking uncomfortable.

'Let her *go*, can't you. She's only a baby,' said Tanya.

'Then what are you doing involving her in your shoplifting, eh? said the man.

'Who says we've been shoplifting? Prove it! We were just having a look round, there's no law against that, is there?' Tanya said furiously. 'And anyway, I keep telling you, the little kid's done nothing. She isn't even *with* me. Let her go home to her mum.'

'You'll get to see your mums after the police have got here,' said the security man.

'I'll get to see my mum, will I?' said Tanya. 'Well, that'll be a surprise.'

They marched us back into *Indigo*. The boy with the blue eyes was standing with his arms folded, shaking his head.

'Yeah, that's them. Stupid kids,' he said.

'You're the one who's the stupid poser,' Tanya yelled. 'We haven't done anything. We were only looking at your crummy stock, trying on the boots and that. We haven't nicked *anything*.'

She went on insisting even when we were taken through to a stockroom at the back. A female security guard came with us and asked us to give her anything we'd taken.

'We haven't taken anything,' Tanya repeated.

I just cried, and Tanya put her arm round me. I could feel she was trembling too, and that made me cry harder.

'Look, kids. Don't make me have to search you,' said the security lady.

'You're not to lay a finger on us! You've got no right. And I keep telling and telling you, we haven't nicked anything. That guy out there, the one who fancies himself, he just wants to get us into trouble,' Tanya insisted.

'He says you took one of their blue hand-knitted sweaters,' said the security lady.

'Then he's a liar,' said Tanya.

But the security lady reached forward and tapped the soft bulge of Tanya's stomach. It slipped. The woman put her hand under Tanya's sweatshirt and pulled. The blue knitted sweater fell out onto the floor.

'Who's the liar?' she said.

'You planted it on me,' said Tanya. 'Didn't she, Mandy? She shoved it at me to frame me, yeah?'

The security men at the door started laughing.

'We've got a right tough little cookie here,' said one. 'I bet when the police come we'll find she's got a lot of previous.'

'The police!' I sobbed.

It was even more scary when they arrived, a man and a woman in dark uniform and police hats.

'Hey, hey! Do I really look so fierce?' said the policeman, laughing. He looked from Tanya to me. 'A little Thelma and Louise, eh?'

'Oh, ha ha. A comedian,' said Tanya.

'Well, you're the hard nut,' said the policeman. He walked towards me. I cowered away from him, snivelling. 'So who's this little shrinking violet, eh?'

'Give over, you're frightening her,' said the policewoman putting her arm round me. 'Don't cry, now. What's your name, eh?'

'Mandy,' I wept.

'And how old are you, Mandy?'

'Ten.'

'She's got nothing to do with this. She's just a little kid who tagged after me,' said Tanya fiercely. 'Let her go.'

The policewoman patted me gently. 'Well, we're certainly not in the habit of taking prisoners as little as you, poppet.'

Tanya hunched herself up small. 'Couldn't you let us both go, please?' she asked, sniffing.

'She's a great little actress,' said the security woman.

But the policewoman seemed to be on our side.

'As both the girls are so young and your property has been recovered, do you still want to go ahead and have us prosecute, sir?' said the policewoman to the boy with the blue eyes.

Tanya and I stared at him pleadingly.

'It's strict *Indigo* policy. Shoplifters are always prosecuted,' he said, folding his arms. 'Half the time it's kids like these two. They're a pest. They need to be taught a lesson.'

'In that case, sir, you'd better come with us to the station and make a full statement there,' said the policeman. 'Now, you say you saw the older girl take the sweater?'

'It's hand-knitted. Sells at £95,' said the boy indignantly.

'You've got expensive taste, young lady,' said the policeman to Tanya. He turned to the security woman. 'And she had this sweater on her when you stopped her?'

'It was stuffed up her own sweatshirt. I could see this little blue cuff hanging down, so I pulled.'

'She should have waited till you lot came before searching me, shouldn't she?' said Tanya. 'You've got no real proof now, have you?'

'We've got proof all right,' said the boy with the blue eyes. 'We've got video cameras installed. We'll have a lovely little film of you stealing our sweater.'

Tanya saw he wasn't fooling. She still didn't give up on my account.

'Then your precious film will show that this little kid here didn't do anything,' she said, pointing to me.

'She was larking around with you. And then she ran off when you did,' said the boy.

'That's not a crime, is it?' said Tanya. 'She's not a thief.'

'But I'm afraid we've got reasonable grounds to think you're a thief, young woman,' said the policeman. 'So I'm therefore arresting you.'

I listened to him cautioning her, the words so familiar from all the police series on the television – and I still couldn't believe it was really happening.

'We're really being arrested!' I whispered.

'We're not arresting you, pet,' said the policewoman. 'You'd better come along to the police station with your friend, and tell us exactly what happened, then we'll get your mum to come and take you home, OK?'

'But you're arresting Tanya?'

'I'm afraid so,' she said.

We had to walk all the way back out of the shopping centre, the policewoman holding me, the policeman holding Tanya. She tried to wriggle and dodge once or twice, but he held her firmly by the shoulders and just laughed at her.

There was a white police patrol car at the back of the shopping centre. More people stared as Tanya and I were put in the back, the policewoman in between us. I was still crying.

'Let me sit next to Mandy,' said Tanya.

'Sorry, love,' said the policewoman.

'But she needs me to hold her,' said Tanya.

'Yes, I know. But you could try and pass something to her, couldn't you?'

'Look.' Tanya waggled her empty hand in front of the policewoman's face. 'See? Empty. So can I at least hold her hand?'

'All right then.'

So we drove to the police station with Tanya holding my hand tight across the policewoman's lap. And all the time her small strong fingers with their bitten nails were clinging to me I felt just a tiny bit braver.

'You could have run off and left me,' I said. 'But you stayed. So I wouldn't be scared on my own.'

'Yeah. Daft, wasn't I?' said Tanya, and she grinned at me.

I saw her looking at the lock in the back of

the car. The policewoman saw her looking too.

'Kiddielocks,' she said. 'So don't try to jump out, pal.'

'Foiled again,' said Tanya, tutting.

She was acting daft, as if it didn't really matter. I knew why. It was to try to make it easier for me. All I could do was grip her hand in gratitude.

Then we got to the police station and even Tanya couldn't grin and act the fool. We were taken across a yard and through a security door and down a dark corridor and into a big room with a desk and a bench.

'The Custody Suite,' said Tanya, looking round.

'Sounds like you've been in one or two already?' said the policewoman.

Tanya gave her a tiny tired smile and sat down heavily on the bench. I sat beside her, huddling up to her.

'Sit further apart, girls,' said a new police-man. 'Now, I'm Sergeant Stockton. I want you both to tell me your names and addresses and then I'll give your parents a ring.'

'What's your mum going to say, Mandy?' said Tanya. 'She'll kill me.'

'What about your own mum?' said Sergeant Stockton sternly.

'Haven't got one,' said Tanya. 'Haven't got a dad either now. He's not considered a fit parent, right? So you want my appropriate adult, yeah?'

The sergeant nodded. 'That's the ticket. Sounds like you could fill in this form quicker than me, young lady. So who is it to be?'

'Well, you'd better phone Pat, my foster mum. She'll be going spare anyway, wondering why we're not back. Now look, Sergeant Stockton. I've got to make something clear.' Tanya got off the bench and went over and stood by his desk. 'I'm going to be absolutely honest.'

'That's right. Make my day,' said the Sergeant.

'No, I'm not messing about. I'm being serious. The little kid over there—'

'You say she's nothing to do with you?'

'Well, she is. Obviously. But she's just the kid over the road. She's looked after by my foster mum while her mum works mornings. She tags round after me. We do go round together. But I swear to you, she's never nicked a thing. She's a real little goody-goody and she comes from a lovely family and she's never ever been in any trouble before. She's only here because of me. So you'll let her go, won't you? You won't even caution her?'

The sergeant smiled at Tanya. 'It's OK. She just needed to be taken to a place of safety. But she can go home as soon as her mum comes.'

'What about Tanya?' I asked. 'Will she be able to go home too?'

'Eventually,' said the sergeant.

'What does that mean?' said Tanya. But it looked as if she knew. She came back and slumped on the bench. She shut her eyes as if she was trying not to cry. This time she wasn't pretending.

I got closer and put my arm round her. The sergeant frowned a little, but let us sit close this time. I held Tanya all the time the sergeant filled out his custody record. She gave all mad made-up answers at first, but she knew that Mrs Williams would be here soon, so she changed her mind and told the truth.

'And now you've got my name and date of birth you can tap into your computer and find out my vast criminal record, eh?' said Tanya.

'Technology at our fingertips,' said the sergeant.

'Juvenile court, here I come,' said Tanya.

'Is that like prison?' I whispered, terrified. 'They won't lock you up, will they? Oh Tanya, I can't stand it if they take you away. I've *got* to keep seeing you.'

'Get real, Mandy,' said Tanya, her shoulders tense under my arm. 'Your mum isn't going to let you come near me now, no matter what.'

Mum was white and shaking when she arrived. Mrs Williams was with her, with the three little boys, all of them whimpering. Tanya sighed deeply. She looked at Mrs Williams. She looked at Mum.

'Sorry,' she said. It came out wrong. I knew she really truly meant it, but it sounded as if she was being cheeky and defiant.

'It's a bit late for saying sorry,' said Mrs Williams.

My mum didn't say anything. But I saw the way she looked at Tanya. I knew Tanya was right.

I started crying again then, because I couldn't bear it. Mum and I were taken to this other room and an inspector came to talk to us.

'You've been a very silly girl, Mandy,' he said solemnly. 'I hope you've learnt your lesson now. You mustn't ever go round with anyone who shoplifts. They'll get into trouble and they'll get *you* into trouble too.'

Then he started talking to Mum – and he treated her as if she was a silly girl too.

'I really feel it's not sensible to let a little girl like Mandy trot round with a tough teenager like Tanya,' he said. 'My advice would be to keep a proper eye on Mandy in future and maybe vet her friends more thoroughly.'

Mum swallowed painfully, bright pink now. She cried too on the way home.

'I can't believe this is happening,' she said, over and over. She kept looking at me and shaking her head and collapsing into fresh tears.

She phoned Dad when we got home and he left the office straightaway. I had the two of them talking to me all afternoon. Saying the same things over and over again. Saying how sad and sorry they were. Saying they felt so ashamed. Saying they couldn't believe how I'd deceived them, going off on these shopping trips with Tanya. Saying they couldn't bear it that I hadn't told them about Tanya's shop-lifting.

Then they started getting cross with each other as well as with me.

'I said over and over again that I didn't want Mandy mixed up with that Tanya,' said Mum. 'But you wouldn't listen to me. You thought you knew best. And now look what's happened!'

'All right, all right.

There's no need to rub it in. I didn't dream it would come to this. I always thought Mandy had enough sense to stick to what she knew was right. If you didn't baby her quite so much then maybe she'd be able to stand up for herself better,' said Dad.

I cried harder and they stopped shouting and Mum mopped my face and Dad got me a drink of water and then they both gave me a cuddle.

'We're terribly upset and disappointed – but we do realize it wasn't all your fault, darling. Don't cry so,' said Mum.

'Come on, little Polly Pigtails, stop the tears. It's all over now,' said Dad.

'But what about *Tanya*?' I sobbed.

'Never mind about Tanya!' said Mum.

'You'll find another friend soon, Mandy,' said Dad.

'But Tanya's my best ever friend! I can still see her, can't I? She won't ever go shoplifting again. She promised she wouldn't anyway, it was just because that boy in *Indigo* was so horrid. But it won't happen again. She hated getting me into trouble too. She tried so hard to get me off. She could have run away and left me but she didn't, she stayed to look after me. Oh, please, you've *got* to understand. I just *have* to see her.'

I kept rushing to the window, waiting for Tanya to come back. A car pulled up outside the

Williams' house late in the afternoon. There was a young woman driving, Mrs Williams and the three boys – and Tanya.

I felt weak with relief. At least they hadn't locked her up somewhere. But she looked awful when she got out the car. She wasn't walking with her usual bounce. Her hair was sticking up on end as if she'd been running her fingers through it.

'I've *got* to see what they're going to do to her,' I said.

But they wouldn't let me. Mum went to see Mrs Williams instead. Mum was very angry with her, because she felt she shouldn't have let me go out round the town with Tanya. I waited desperately for her to come back. Mum was gone quite a while. And when she came back she looked strange. Startled.

'What is it, Mum? What's going to happen to Tanya? Has she got to go to court?'

Mum nodded. 'Thank goodness you're not going to be involved at all, Mandy.'

'I thought they'd just caution her,' said Dad.

'Apparently she's had lots of cautions already. They're going to take a full case history and take all her background into consideration. It's likely to take weeks,' said Mum.

'So she'll be home here for weeks?' I said.

Mum put her arm round me. 'No, dear,

Tanya isn't going to be here,' she said. 'She's going to go to a children's home. Pat Williams feels she can't cope. I can see she's got a point. She was talked into fostering Tanya and she always made it plain she'd have to go if there was any trouble. I mean, she's got those little boys to think about.'

'So she's just washing her hands of Tanya?' said Dad, sounding shocked.

'What else can she do?' said Mum.

'If I'd stolen that jumper would you get rid of me?' I said.

'Don't be so silly, Mandy.'

'But *would* you?'

'No, of course not. You know we wouldn't. We love you and we'll go on loving you no matter what you do,' said Mum.

'But no-one loves poor old Tanya,' said Dad.

'*I* love her!' I said. 'When has she got to go?'

'Well, right now,' said Mum. 'It does seem a bit . . . but I suppose there's no point dragging these things out. Her social worker's there now, helping her get her bag packed.'

'She's going *now*?' I said. 'Then I've got to say goodbye to her.'

'No, you're not going near her,' said Mum.

'It's maybe not a good idea, Mandy,' said Dad.

'I'll just say goodbye,' I said. 'I've got to. You can't stop me.'

There was a pile of my things on the living room table, puzzles and books and my big tin of felt-tips. I peered at them desperately and then grabbed the rainbow pens. I was out of the living room, down the hall and out the front door before Mum and Dad realized what was happening.

Dad caught me up as I was hammering on Mrs Williams' door. 'Now, Mandy, come on, come back home,' he said.

Mrs Williams answered the door and stared at us.

'Is Tanya really going?' I said.

Mrs Williams nodded, looking dazed.

'It's for the best,' she said, though she didn't look certain.

'Can I say goodbye?' I begged.

Mrs Williams looked at Dad.

'Oh, all right,' said Dad. 'Go on, be quick. I'll wait here.'

I went charging up the stairs and into Tanya's bedroom. The social worker lady was there, scooping Tanya's stuff into a big plastic bag. Tanya was sitting on her bed, not helping.

'Hi, Mandy,' said Tanya flatly.

'Oh, Tanya!' I said, rushing to her. 'You're going?'

Her fists were clenched. Her face looked clenched too.

'Yeah, I'm going. Pat's booting me out,' said Tanya.

'Come on now, Tanya. You know you were only here on a temporary basis,' said the social worker. 'And we'll work really hard to get you a new placement. Anyway, it's not so bad in this new children's home.'

'It'll be a dump,' said Tanya. 'They all are. Because they're dumping grounds. For kids nobody wants.'

'I want you, Tanya!' I said.

She gave me a sad little smile. 'Hey, I want to say goodbye to my friend,' she said to the social worker. 'How about giving us two minutes alone together, eh?'

The social worker straightened up and sighed. 'OK. *One* minute. I need to sort some stuff out with Mrs Williams anyway.'

She went out the room. Tanya and I sat together on her bed. I tried desperately hard to think of the right thing to say but there weren't any words.

'Oh, Tanya,' I said, and then I hugged her so hard I nearly knocked her over. The tin of felt-tips slid off the bed and sprinkled rainbow colours all over the carpet.

'Hey, watch it!' said Tanya. 'Now look what you've done.' She gave me a little pat and then

wriggled free. 'Let's get them all picked up. You
don't want to lose any, do you? What did you
bring them over for anyway? It's not like we've
got time to do any colouring.'

I knelt down too, feeling for the felt-tips that
had rolled under the bed.

'They're for you, Tanya,' I said. 'A goodbye
present.'

'What? All of them?' said Tanya.

'Well, one or two won't be much good by
themselves,' I said, giving her a little poke.
'Yes. All of them.'

'Are you sure? You can't give me your
rainbow felt-tips. What will your mum say?'

'It's not up to my mum. They're mine, so it's
up to me. And I want you to have them.'

'Oh, Mandy. No-one's ever given me such a
lovely present,' said Tanya. She rubbed her
eyes. They already looked sore, with purple
shadows underneath. I didn't know if it was her

make-up, or because she was so sad. But she managed another smile. 'Keep looking, there's a green and a blue still missing. I want a totally complete perfect set of felt-tip pens, thanks very much!'

We found the green and the blue and slotted them into place. Tanya ran her finger over all the pens so that they played a strange little tune.

'Mine,' she said. Then she looked round the room. She poked about in her half-full plastic bag. 'I'd better find a present for you, eh?'

'No, it's all right. Honestly. Anyway you've given me lots of stuff. The velvet scrunchie and—'

'I want to give you something special. Seeing as your rainbow felt-tips were probably your very best thing.' Tanya tipped the plastic bag up and emptied it onto the carpet. She scrabbled and then seized something triumphantly. Her violet sequin sparkly top.

'Here! You have it, Mandy.'

'But I can't. It's your special top.'

'That's why I want you to have it. My best thing for my best friend,' said Tanya.

We had one last hug.

And then we had to say goodbye.

RAINBOW

Rainbow

I couldn't believe Tanya was gone. I kept thinking of things I had to tell her – and then remembering. Every time I heard footsteps out in the street I leapt to the window, even though I knew it couldn't possibly be her.

I couldn't settle to anything at all. I couldn't even play Miranda Rainbow. I was stuck being me, Mandy White, and I couldn't stand it.

Mum and Dad tried hard to distract me. Mum even bought me a big new tin of rainbow felt-tips without a murmur. 'It was very sweet of you to give Tanya your other set,' she said.

'You didn't even want me to say goodbye to her,' I said.

'I was still in a state of shock after having to collect you from the police,' said Mum.

'You never liked Tanya, though. You didn't ever want me to see her,' I said fiercely.

'You're being a bit hard on your mum,' said Dad. 'We only said you couldn't see her after the shoplifting business. And it's silly to say we didn't like her. She was a smashing girl in many ways, so lively, and basically good-hearted—'

'She *is*. Don't talk about her as if she's dead,' I said. 'She's still my best ever friend, you know, even though she's gone. And Mum didn't ever want us to be friends, did you?'

'Now, now,' said Mum. 'All right, I didn't think it was very sensible. And I was proved right, too. But there's no need to look at me like that, Mandy. I didn't have anything against Tanya personally. It's just that she wasn't the right age for you, and she didn't come from the right sort of background.'

'Melanie is the right age, the right background, you thought she was the right sort of friend for me. And she was ever so mean to me and ganged up with Kim and Sarah against me. They were hateful. Tanya was always lovely to me.'

I didn't just say it. I shouted it. I thought they'd get cross then. But they just stared at each other, looking helpless.

'That's a good point, Mandy,' said Dad, sighing.

'It's not as simple as that,' said Mum. 'But I

wish I'd tried a bit harder with Tanya.'

'It's easy to say that now, when she's been taken away,' I said.

I stamped off to my room and slammed the door. I lay on my bed for a while, clutching Olivia Orang-Utan, pretending her orange fur was Tanya's hair. Then I sat up and dressed her in Tanya's violet sequin top. It fell way past her paws, an amazing evening gown.

I tried on the top myself. I took off my glasses and peered short-sightedly into the mirror. I could just see a swirl of purple sequins. I could kid myself I looked amazingly glamorous, a real Miranda Rainbow. But then I put my glasses back on and everything shifted into focus. I was Mandy White again, and I went in and out in all the wrong places. The violet top puckered loosely over my flat chest and showed off my babyish round tummy.

'Mandy?' It was Mum, knocking at my bedroom door.

I tried to rip the top off quickly, because I couldn't stand the thought of Mum laughing at me. My head got caught and when I pulled, my glasses went flying. They fell with a clatter on my chest of drawers and broke in two again.

'Oh, no!'

'What's the matter, Mandy?' said Mum, coming in.

'My glasses! They've broken again.'

'Well, we'll see if Daddy can fix them with Superglue like he did last time. But I think we'll have to get you a new pair some time this summer,' said Mum.

'Really grown-up fashionable glasses?' I asked.

'Yes. So long as they're not too expensive.'

'And can I have my hair cut so that they won't look stupid with my baby plaits?'

'Mmm. I'm not so sure about that,' said Mum. 'If it's really important to you then maybe you can. I suppose it's your own hair after all.' Mum paused. 'But I tell you one thing I am sure about, Mandy. I don't want you wearing that purple sequin top. Certainly not outdoors.'

'It doesn't fit right, anyway,' I said. 'But it looked lovely on Tanya.'

'Well,' said Mum.

'I miss her so,' I said. 'She said she'd write,

but she hates writing, so I don't think she will.'

'I know you're missing her, darling. And I understand. But believe me, you'll make some other friends soon. Tell you what, why don't you get in touch with that nice boy who rang you up after the accident? Arthur.'

'No! I couldn't. I'd feel stupid.'

'I'll get in touch with his mother if you like.'

'No, Mum! I don't *want* to. I don't want to do anything,' I insisted.

Dad took time off work and kept suggesting we go to the pictures or the park. He spent one day taking me round the museums in London and I pretended I was enjoying myself – but I'd have been just as happy lying on my bed at home doing nothing.

Mum scoured the local newspaper for holiday activities and eventually talked me into signing up for a story-writing session at the library.

She took me shopping on Saturday and said I could have new glasses. I tried on hundreds of pairs: tiny owly ones, great big bold specs, glittery party glasses. I wished Tanya was there to tell me which suited me most. Mum liked a baby pink pair with a little white rabbit at either end. I knew I never wanted to wear anything with a rabbit on it ever again. Particularly in pink.

'But pink suits you so, Mandy,' said Mum.

'Not pink, Mum. Any other colour. Red. Orange. Purple.'

I peered through glasses all the colours of the rainbow. And then I spotted a perfect pair. Not too little. Not too large. With striped frames. Rainbow stripes. Red, orange, yellow, green, blue, indigo, violet.

'Oh, Mum! I like these best. Can I have the rainbow glasses?'

They weren't too expensive so Mum said yes. We went and had an ice cream in Maxwell's while we were waiting for my glasses to be made up with the right lenses for me. I chose a strawberry special, sprinkled with rainbow dots. Mum had one too, even though she was supposed to be on another diet.

'I wish I'd taken Tanya here now,' said Mum.

We finished our strawberry specials in silence.

Mum decided to chance going into work late the next Monday so she could deliver me at the library for the writing session. She wanted to come in with me but I wouldn't let her, in case any of the children thought me a baby.

I needn't have worried. There was only one other person my age. Arthur!

He was already sitting at a table at the back of the room with two other boys. There wasn't a spare chair at his table. And I didn't want him to think I was being pushy. He didn't seem all that thrilled to see me there. He just nodded nervously at me, going pink.

I didn't want to embarrass him further in front of the other boys. They were maybe his friends.

I didn't know who to sit with. I didn't want to squash up with the very little ones printing in wobbly wax crayon.

There were two girls about seven at another table.

'Maybe you'd like to sit with Sarah and Julie and work on their Woodland Bunny story with them?' said the library lady.

'No, thank you,' I said. 'I don't really want to write about rabbits. I'll make up my own story.'

I sat at a little table by myself. The library lady offered me paper and pencils and wax crayons, but I had my own drawing book and my new tin of rainbow felt-tips with me. Arthur was looking at me so I hurriedly started writing. I didn't want him to think I was trying to catch his eye.

I wrote down the special story Tanya and I had made up together, about Love Tanyanita and Miranda Rainbow sharing a flat together. It made me feel very lonely and sad remembering it. I kept hearing Tanya's voice as she made it all up.

'Are you all right, Mandy?' the library lady asked, bending over me.

'Yes, I'm fine,' I said, feeling stupid. I put my arm over my page. I didn't want her to read our private story.

She moved on to the boys' table at the back. The boys who weren't Arthur were scribbling stories based on video games. They'd got a bit bored and were flicking rubbers at each other, going Zap and Pow and Kerplunk. The library lady sighed and skirted round them towards Arthur.

'What are you writing today, Arthur?' she said, smiling expectantly. Arthur was obviously a regular at the story-writing sessions.

The Zap-Pow-Kerplunk boys rolled their eyes and made gagging gestures.

'It's nothing. It's just . . . No, honestly,' Arthur mumbled.

'"The Knight Who Wouldn't Fight",' the library lady read out loud.

'The knight who wouldn't fight!' said Zap.

'What a dumb wimpy title,' said Pow.

'By a dumb wimpy boy,' said Zap.

'Dumb, wimpy, nitty-Knighty Arthur,' said Pow.

'Now then, you two, stop being so silly,' said the library lady. 'Don't take any notice of them, Arthur.'

Arthur said nothing. He didn't look at the boys. He didn't look at the library lady. He didn't look at me.

I looked at him properly through my new rainbow glasses. Then I got up and walked over to his table.

'Can I see what you've written, Arthur?' I said. 'Here, I bet those two haven't even heard of King Arthur and all the knights of the round table. They're still way down at the Super Mario and Sonic stage.'

Zap and Pow spluttered and squealed. The library lady blinked. Arthur went bright red. But he pushed his book towards me.

'Here,' he said. He sounded gruff. But I knew it was OK.

I got my chair and sat at his table for a bit, but Zap and Pow kept bombarding us with rubbers and jogging us whenever we wrote, so Arthur and I moved over to my little table.

I decided I wanted to go to the story-writing sessions all week. Arthur and I sat together every day. We started to work on a new story together, about a beautiful medieval witch, Mandiana the Magic, and an all-powerful wizard called Dark Art. We took turns writing the story and drew a picture for every page and coloured it all in with my rainbow felt-tips.

I knew that Arthur was pleased I'd turned up at the library out of the blue. He hadn't said much because he was shy, like me. He didn't want me to think *he* was pushy.

Arthur's mum came to meet him at lunchtimes. She studied in the library archives while we did our writing class. She had the same pale face and untidy fringe as Arthur. They even wore identical navy anoraks. She was a different sort of mum but ever so interesting when you talked to her. She gave us some brilliant ideas for evil spells and knew all about poisonous potions and herbs.

My mum got on well with Arthur's mum. They made friends too. Arthur's mum said I was very welcome to go round to their house in the mornings when the writing sessions stopped.

'That would be good, eh, Mandy?' said Arthur, going pink again.

'Yeah. Right,' I said.

It wouldn't be as good as being with Tanya of course. Nowhere near. But Arthur was OK. He was a friend.

But I didn't go to the Kings' house the next week after all.

I knew something terrible had happened when Mum came to collect me on Friday. Her eyes were red and her face was all puffy. My tummy went tight.

'Mum, what's wrong?'

She tried hard to be brave in front of Mrs King and Arthur.

'Nothing's really wrong, dear. I've just had a little shock, that's all.'

'Have you heard something awful about Tanya?'

Mum stared at me as if I was mad.

'No, of course not. No, I've just been forced to join the massed ranks of the unemployed,' said Mum.

She was talking in such a strange way I didn't get what she meant at first. But then

164

when Mrs King started talking very sympa-
thetically about redundancy I realized. Mum
had lost her job.

When we were indoors, away from the Kings,
her face went wobbly and she started crying
again.

'Don't cry, Mum,' I said timidly.

She cried harder, her eyes screwed up, her
mouth open. I'd never seen her cry that way
before. It made me feel awful and embarrassed
and scared.

Mum went up to her bedroom and I hung
back for a minute and then followed her worriedly. She'd taken her good suit off and was
lying on top of her duvet in her petticoat, crying
and crying.

'Mum?' I said, and I sat down gingerly on the
edge of the bed.

I reached out and patted her soft, shaking shoulder.

'Oh, Mandy,' Mum sobbed, and then she scrabbled around for a hankie and tried hard to stop crying. 'I'm sorry, darling. Don't look so worried. It's not the end of the world. I don't know why I'm making such a fuss.' Her voice wavered up and down, and every so often there was a sob she couldn't stop, like a hiccup.

'You'll get another job, Mum,' I said.

Mum shook her head. 'I'm not so sure, Mandy. Oh dear, it was so awful. I had to clear my desk and get out straightaway. I couldn't believe it was really happening. Everyone looked at me as if I'd got some horrible disease. My boss said it was because I was unreliable. He kept on about all the time off I'd had, what with my teeth playing up and then when I had to look after you—'

'So it's my fault?' I said.

'No, no! Of course not, Mandy. And anyway, he was just using that as an excuse. He practically admitted it. He said I didn't really fit into a busy modern office. My way of thinking was all wrong. He said I was too old-fashioned. But what he really meant was that I was too *old*.'

'Oh, Mum. You're not old. Well. Not *that* old.'

'Yes, I am,' said Mum. She blew her nose and sat up properly. 'Goodness, I must look a sight. I *am* old, Mandy. When I look at the other mums down at your school I can't help realizing I'm old enough to be *their* mum.'

'You're not anyone else's mum but mine,' I said, and I put my arms round her.

Mum went after lots of jobs that summer but for a long time she kept getting turned down. She got very depressed and she even started to get thinner, because she didn't feel like eating much. I'd always longed for Mum to stop being so fat, but now I wasn't sure. It was as if the Mum I knew was slowly wearing away, like a bar of soap. I wanted her really big and really bossy again, because that was the way she was supposed to be.

But it was OK after all. The week before I started back at school Mum got another job. She'd gone after an office job in Maxwell's, but she hadn't been able to cope with their computer. They suggested she apply as one of their part-time sales staff instead. She got a job going in Ladies' Separates, and she took me for enormous knickerbocker glories in Maxwell's soda fountain to celebrate.

'It's a lovely department. I like the look of the ladies I'll be working with. It's less money, but I'll get a good discount on goods, even though I'm only part-time,' said Mum, licking ice cream from her lips and scraping her tall glass. 'Pity I don't get discounts on ice creams, eh?'

Mum was happy again. I wished I could feel happy too. I still missed Tanya so much. I had Arthur now, but he wasn't the same. And school was starting on Monday, and I'd begun to have nightmares about Kim and Melanie and Sarah.

I kept telling myself it was a new school year, a new class, a new start. But I still felt sick and sweaty when I walked into school. Kim and Melanie and Sarah were already in the classroom, at the back. Kim whispered something and they all burst out laughing, looking at me.

It was starting again. I stood still, not knowing where to sit. All the girls had friends already. I was stuck without anyone.

Arthur was sitting right at the front. He tapped the desk next to him.

'Hey, Mandy. Come and sit here,' he said.

I stared at him. None of the girls ever sat with the boys. You just never did it, not in our class.

'I can't sit next to you, Arthur,' I hissed 'You're a boy.'

'Brilliant deduction!'

said Arthur, raising his eyebrows. 'So what?'

I thought about it. So what, indeed? I sat next to Arthur. Kim and Melanie and Sarah giggled and sneered. Some of the boys wolf-whistled and made stupid remarks.

'Nutters,' said Arthur.

'Nutters,' I agreed.

'They're the nutty ones,' said Kim. 'Two swotty little twits. They're just sticking together because they haven't got any other friends.'

She went on and on, but her words were just like little pinpricks, not great big daggers. I knew it wasn't true. I did have friends. I had Tanya, who was the best friend in all the world. And I had Arthur.

We stayed sitting together at the front, and the new Year Six teacher Miss Moseley didn't mind at all.

Kim and Melanie and Sarah sat in a three-some at the back, all crammed together. Miss Moseley wasn't having any of that.

'Come on, you three. You haven't got room to work all squashed up like that. One of you had better pop over to a spare table.'

Melanie and Sarah looked at Kim plead-ingly, both desperate to stay with her. Kim sat back, smiling, looking from one to the other. We all craned round to see who she was going to pick and who she was going to send packing.

'Kim?' said Miss Moseley. She knew her name already. Everyone in the whole school knew Kim. 'You go and sit at the spare table, please.'

We all stared at Miss Moseley, astonished. She didn't understand. Or maybe she understood all too well.

'No, I'll stay here,' said Kim. 'Melanie can sit at the spare table. Or Sarah.'

Melanie and Sarah looked agonized.

'I want to stay with you, Kim,' said Melanie.

'No, I've got to stay, I've been your friend much longer,' said Sarah.

'It's not up to Kim,' said Miss Moseley briskly. 'I'm the teacher and I say who sits where. Melanie and Sarah, stay where you are. Kim. You move to the spare table.' She paused. '*At once!*'

Kim got to her feet and moved all her things to the spare table. She had two bright pink spots on her cheeks. She glared at Miss Moseley.

Miss Moseley smiled. 'Right. Now we're all sorted out and sitting comfortably, we can start our lesson.'

We were all still a bit stunned. Miss Moseley was young with fluffy fair hair and she often wore fluffy pastel jumpers. We'd thought she was all soft and fluffy too. We'd got it wrong. She was as strong as steel.

I decided I was going to like it in Year Six with Miss Moseley. We started all sorts of new lessons. We were doing the Victorians all that first term and we all had to choose one special aspect to study with a partner. Arthur and I decided to do a project about this group of Victorian painters who liked doing pictures of King Arthur and all his knights and various damsels in distress. The others in the class chose stuff like Childhood or Servants or Fashion or Railways. Miss Moseley was very pleased with Arthur and me. She said we'd started a very original and interesting project.

Kim made vomit noises. Miss Moseley raised her eyebrows but she didn't bother to get cross. She didn't seem to think Kim was particularly important.

We had one brand new subject in Year Six. It was down on our timetable for Friday afternoon. It was called Circle Time. We weren't quite sure what it was.

'Maybe we'll draw circles with protractors,' said Arthur, getting his protractor out of his pencil case.

'What, to make patterns? I like doing that,' I said. 'And then we can colour them in.'

But we didn't draw circles in Circle Time. We made the circle ourselves, pushing the tables back and sitting round on our chairs. Miss Moseley sat in the circle too. Kim could sit in between Melanie and Sarah again. She barged between them. Arthur and I sat next to each other of course.

'Circle Time is going to be our special time, when we sit round together as a class and talk about all sorts of different things,' said Miss Moseley.

'Oooh, she's going to tell us about sex,' said Kim, and everyone giggled.

Miss Moseley laughed too.

'Not today, folks. So you can all simmer down. Circle Time is when we discuss various issues.'

'What's an issue, Miss Moseley?'

'Issue! Issue!' said Kim, pretending to sneeze.

'An issue is something currently on our minds. Something we want to talk about . . .'

'Like *Neighbours*?'

'No, not exactly. But all sorts of issues are dealt with in *Neighbours*. Anyway. Today in Circle Time I thought we'd talk about bullying,' said Miss Moseley.

There was a sudden silence. Everyone looked

at Kim. Her cheeks went pink with the Dutch doll spots. People were looking at Melanie and Sarah too. And me. I started to feel sick. I didn't want to talk about it. And if Kim and Melanie and Sarah got told off they'd think I'd been telling tales on them. I stared at Miss Moseley. She was going to make it worse.

But Miss Moseley smiled at me, smiled at everyone, calm and composed, her fair hair standing out around her face like a golden halo. She took out a newspaper and read to us about a boy who had been beaten up by three other boys at his school. She showed us the photo of his poor bruised face. We all agreed that this was awful. Then she read to us about a girl who kept getting punched and kicked until she was so scared of going to school that she hanged herself. We discussed this too. Miss Moseley asked us to think how the boy and girl must have felt. It started to get really sad and scary.

'I don't want to think about that girl hanging herself. It'll give me nightmares,' said Melanie.

'I know it's very uncomfortable thinking about it. But you're all getting older and much more sensible now you're in Year Six. You're ready to discuss very painful grown-up topics. Now, what do you all think we should do about bullies like this?'

'They should get beaten up, too.'

'They should get locked up.'

'No-one should ever talk to them ever again.'

People's suggestions started to get fiercer and fiercer.

'This isn't always possible, or indeed practical,' said Miss Moseley. 'And I think we have to try to work out *why* people bully. Then we can maybe stop it before it gets too much of a habit. So. Why do *you* think people bully?'

'Because they're big and they want to hurt.'

'Because they're nasty.'

'Because they like getting people scared.'

'Yes. These are all sensible suggestions. But try to think a bit deeper. Are bullies happy people?' Miss Moseley asked.

'They're happy when they hurt.'

'Yes, I suppose so. But think about it. Think about when you're very very happy. Say it's your birthday and all your family and friends

have given you a big hug and some lovely presents and you feel really great. Now. Do you
want to hurt anyone when you're in that sort of
situation?'

We thought – and shook our heads.

'Of course not. You just want to be nice to
people. But suppose you've had a really bad day
and got into trouble at school and your friend's
gone off with someone else and your mum and
dad are cross and they've given your little sister
a treat and yet they just tell you off . . . Do you
want to be nice to people now? Or do you feel
like being nasty?'

'Nasty!' we said.

'Of course you do. So if your little sister
comes and starts showing off, you maybe give
her a little push, or tell her she's stupid, right?'

Most people nodded, laughing.

'But that's not real bullying. I mean, I can't
stick *my* sister, but I wouldn't kick her head in
or make her kill herself.'

People laughed more, but Miss Moseley was
looking serious.

'That's exactly it, though. Bullying isn't
always terribly dramatic and dreadful, with
people seriously hurt or even dying. We're all
very thankful nothing like that happens in our
school. But I'm sure we can all think of various
occasions when a group of us have picked on
another one?'

No-one was laughing now. My tummy went tight again.

'One person gets picked on, and it starts to be a habit. And others join in. Because everyone wants to side with the bully so that *they* don't get picked on.'

'Sometimes they ask for it. Because they're *stupid*,' someone muttered. It could have been Kim.

Miss Moseley had very sharp ears under her fluffy hair.

'No-one ever asks to be bullied,' she said. 'But you're right, sometimes people get bullied because they're stupid. Though that's not a very kind word. People can't help it if they're not very bright. And that's a terrible reason for bullying someone, just because they're not clever.'

'And other times someone can get bullied because they're *ever* so clever,' Arthur said suddenly. 'Say they come top of the class and the bully doesn't like it because they're clever too and *they* want to be top.'

Miss Moseley nodded.

'That's very shrewd of you, Arthur.'

Some of the others were whispering and nudging each other. I heard the word Kim several times. And Mandy.

'We won't mention any names,' said Miss

Moseley. 'Remember, this is a *general* discussion.'

Melanie and Sarah were fidgeting. Kim's cheeks were strawberry pink.

'If someone is being bullied you should always tell,' said Miss Moseley, her eyes swivelling round the whole circle. 'Tell your mum and dad. Tell your teacher. Tell another teacher if things still don't get sorted out. The person who is getting bullied needs help. And the person doing the bullying needs help too, because they're sad, sick, silly people. We should feel sorry for them, even though they hurt and do a lot of harm. Even name-calling and silly teasing can be horribly upsetting, can't it?' She looked round the circle again. 'You know what I mean. Pulling silly faces and going chitter-chatter, like a lot of monkeys at the zoo. Bullies are like baboons, those big monkeys with weird faces and bright red bottoms.'

Everyone burst out laughing hearing Miss Moseley say the word bottom.

'The biggest baboon screams a lot and bites all the little ones. All the other big baboons copy, screeching and scratching for fleas. Now, no-one here in my class wants to act like a bully baboon with a bright red bottom, do they?'

Everyone shook their heads – even Melanie and Sarah. Kim's head was bent.

She kept right out of my way after that. She didn't ever wait to get me after school again. She'd have been by herself anyway. Melanie and Sarah didn't want to be her friend any more. They went round just the two of them instead.

Melanie asked if I wanted to make friends again. I said OK but I couldn't be her *best* friend. I had Arthur now anyway. We stayed sitting together in school and we played together in the dinner break and we always walked home together as far as the bus stop. Mum still came to meet me most days, but I didn't mind now that no-one teased me about it.

I still couldn't help hoping that somehow one day Tanya might come running down the road too, in her shorts and clacky sandals. I'd heard from her at last. Just one postcard, and she hadn't put an address.

Hi Mandy
I sed Id rit. The Juv. Cort was a dodel. I jest got a soopervison order. Grat, eh? And I think Im geting a new Foster Mum so things are luking up.
See you, best frend.
Lots of lov
Tanya x x x

See you. I had to keep hoping that I really would see her again some day. If she didn't come back to see me then I'd simply have to go looking for her when I was a bit older. We were still best ever friends. We had to meet up again. Somewhere . . .

ABOUT THE AUTHOR

JACQUELINE WILSON was born in Bath in 1945, but
has spent most of her life in Kingston-on-Thames, Surrey.
She always wanted to be a writer and wrote her first 'novel'
when she was nine, filling countless Woolworths' exercise
books as she grew up. She started work at a publishing
company and then went on to work as a journalist on
Jackie magazine (which was named after her) before
turning to writing fiction full-time.

Since 1990 Jacqueline has written prolifically for children
and has won many of the UK's top awards for children's
books, including the Smarties Prize in 2000
and the Guardian Children's Fiction Award and the
Children's Book of the Year in 1999. Jacqueline was
awarded an OBE in the Queen's Birthday Honours
list, in Golden Jubilee Year, 2002.

Over 10 million copies of Jacqueline's books have now
been sold in the UK and approximately 50,000 copies
of her books are sold each month. An avid reader
herself, Jacqueline has a personal collection of
more than 15,000 books.

She has one grown-up daughter.

*'A brilliant young writer of wit and subtlety whose stories
are never patronising and are often complex and many-
layered'*
THE TIMES

*'Jacqueline Wilson has a rare gift for writing lightly and
amusingly about emotional issues'*
BOOKSELLER

*'Wilson writes like a child, and children instantly recognize
themselves in her characters. The tone of voice is faultless,
her stories are about the problems many children face, and
her plots work with classic simplicity . . . a subtle art is
concealed by artlessness, and some might call that genius'*
DAILY TELEGRAPH

THE STORY OF TRACY BEAKER
Jacqueline Wilson

*I'm Tracy Beaker. This is a book all about
me. I'd read it if I were you. It's the most
incredible dynamic heart-rending story.
Honest.*

Tracy is ten years old. She lives in a
Children's Home but would like a real home
one day, with a real family. Meet Tracy,
follow her story, and share her hopes for the
future in this beautifully observed,
touching, and often very funny tale, all told
in Tracy's own words.

**'Both entertaining and moving. A book
that lingers in the mind long after
it is put down'**
Guardian

0 440 862795

CORGI YEARLING BOOKS

DOUBLE ACT
Jacqueline Wilson

No-one can ever be like a mother to us.
NO-ONE. NO-ONE AT ALL. ESPECIALLY
NOT STUPID FRIZZY DIZZY ROSE.

Ruby and Garnet are ten-year-old twins.
Identical. They do *everything* together,
especially since their mother died two
years earlier. But can being a double
act work for ever? When so much
around them is changing . . .

Winner of the Smarties Prize
Winner of the Children's Book Award
Highly commended for the Carnegie Medal

'Another winner by Jacqueline Wilson
. . . impossible to put down'
School Librarian

'An exuberant story . . . irresistible'
Guardian

'Written with enormous vitality and
wit . . . the story never falters'
Junior Education

0 440 863341

CORGI YEARLING BOOKS

THE LOTTIE PROJECT
Jacqueline Wilson

I don't want to do a boring old project.
Who wants to be like everyone else?
I'm doing a diary . . .

Hi! I'm Charlie (DON'T call me Charlotte –
ever!). History is boring, right? Wrong! The
Victorians weren't all deadly dull and
drippy. Lottie certainly isn't. She's eleven –
like me – but she's left school and has a job
as a nursery maid. Her life is really hard,
just work work work, but I bet she'd know
what to do about my mum's awful boyfriend
and his wimpy little son. I bet she wouldn't
mess it all up like I do . . .

'Vivid, superbly observed story of real life'
The Times

0 440 86366X

CORGI YEARLING BOOKS

THE ILLUSTRATED MUM
Jacqueline Wilson

Star used to love Marigold, love me, love our life together. We three were the colourful ones, like the glowing pictures inked all over Marigold . . .

Covered from head to foot with glorious tattoos, Marigold is the brightest, most beautiful mother in the world. That's what Dolphin thinks (she just wishes her beautiful mum wouldn't stay out partying all night or go *weird* now and then). Her older sister, Star, isn't so sure any more. She loves Marigold too, but sometimes she just can't help wishing she were more *normal* . . .

A powerful and memorable tale for older readers from Jacqueline Wilson, the award-winning author of *The Suitcase Kid*, *Double Act*, *Bad Girls* and many other titles.

'Disturbingly perceptive and provocative'
Guardian

'A marvellous, poignant tale . . . Jacqueline Wilson's best yet'
The Telegraph

WINNER OF THE CHILDREN'S BOOK OF THE YEAR AWARD AND THE GUARDIAN CHILDREN'S FICTION AWARD. SHORT-LISTED FOR THE WHITBREAD AWARD.

0 440 863686

CORGI YEARLING BOOKS

Join the FREE online

Jacqueline Wilson

✿ FAN CLUB ✿

Read Jacqueline's monthly diary, look up

tour info, receive fan club e-newsletters.

All this and more, including members'

jokes and loads of exclusive top offers

Visit www.jacquelinewilson.co.uk

for more info!